P.

Jackson

Shoeless
Joe Jackson
Comes to
Iowa

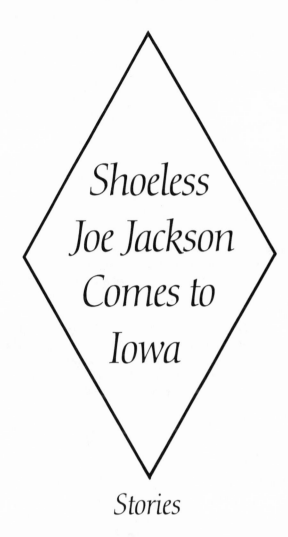

*Shoeless
Joe Jackson
Comes to
Iowa*

Stories

W·P·Kinsella

Southern Methodist University Press
Dallas

Copyright © 1980 by W. P. Kinsella
Published by arrangement with Oberon Press
First Southern Methodist University Press edition, 1993

"Fiona the First" and "The Grecian Urn" first appeared
in *Malahat Review,* "A Quite Incredible Dance" in *Martlet,*
"Shoeless Joe Jackson Comes to Iowa" in *Aurora,* "Waiting
for the Call" in *Story Quarterly,* "Mankiewitz Won't Be
Bowling Tuesday Nights Anymore" in *Sound & Fury,* and
"First Names and Empty Pockets" in *Descant.*

Library of Congress Cataloging-in-Publication Data
Kinsella, W. P.
    Shoeless Joe Jackson comes to Iowa : stories / W. P. Kinsella.—
1st Southern Methodist University Press ed.
        p.   cm.
    ISBN 0-87074-355-4. — ISBN 0-87074-356-2 (pbk.)
    I. Title.
PR9199.3.K443S5   1993
813'.54—dc20   93-3935

Printed in the United States of America

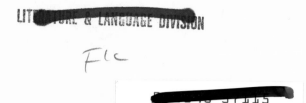
For my daughter, Shannon Leah

Contents

Fiona
the
First

CHAPTER ONE

How to pick up a girl from Grants Pass,
Oregon, in the Los Angeles International Airport

"*T*here are, indeed, dark bargains struck," I said to the
cashier as I paid for my coffee. She looked up, noticed that
there was a person attached to the hand that proffered the exact change, shrugged, and rang up the sale in triplicate as the
accounting firm for the Los Angeles International Airport requires. She was not fazed by my statement, in fact she tried,
and except that her left eyebrow involuntarily lifted about one-
quarter of an inch, succeeded in pretending that customers often said, "There are, indeed, dark bargains struck," when they
paid for their coffee.

In the instant her eyebrow was lifting, she was probably de-
ciding that I looked harmless, virtually everyone decides that,

1

and that I was likely a hungover aluminum window salesman from Lexington, Kentucky, on his way home after a none-too-successful business trip. Which, indeed, I was.

It is not bad work if you can get it: picking up girls in the Los Angeles International Airport. I have been at it for over eighty years. Not always here, of course. I used to frequent the railway station, when railroads were the vortex of mass transportation, and before that the Wells Fargo and Pony Express offices, opening stagecoach doors and offering directions to visitors, female visitors, all the time looking helpful.

I checked my notebook: black, dog-eared, comfortable as a lover of long intimacy. I am now on my way through the alphabet for the second time. It is really surprising how many girls' names there are. Fay, Francene, Gaylene, one covers a lot of ground in eighty years. Today it will be Fiona, and, as always, I am not entirely sure how I decided that. I am not functioning as well as I usually do, possibly it has something to do with the quart of orange juice I drank with breakfast. Corrosive, they tell me. I try to decide, or perhaps remember, if she will be Fiona the first. My thoughts are of Evangeline and orange pulp.

On this very spot, as a child, I fell off the back of a giant auk. Who would believe that? I will test the cashier with it the next time, or test Fiona, if she is a game player. So few are. It is television. Nothing surprises them anymore. I think the thirties and forties were the best; girls still believed in romance. Once, long ago, dressed in black and silver, like Valentino out of a movie, I rode into the Los Angeles Railway Station on a white horse and swept away a girl named . . .

But, to work, to work, today it is Fiona, and since nothing tells me differently, she will be Fiona the first.

A flight is arriving from San Francisco. It bears scrutiny, since many passengers transfer to other flights. I will be there looking helpful. I do hope I find her early today. I hate having to wait for the late evening flights, my feet get tired, I drink too much coffee, smoke too many cigarettes. I get to feeling like a hotel detective.

There she is. Looks like she's been washed up on a sandbar. Lost in the great lonely airport. Mauve. My favorite color. Like a dyed Easter chick from a department store display, a mauve jelly bean trapped in a suitcase fort, she stands, bristling with baggage tags and schedules. Poor thing, something has gone wrong. I can almost touch the hysteria, the air is charged with tears. A mauve scarf in her yellow hair, a yellow sweater, mauve pants with a bib and straps over her shoulders, make her look like a schoolgirl, although she must be twenty-five and is wearing a wedding band.

I stand by, looking helpful as a basset. How should I approach her? What would appeal to her? Gangster? Gunfighter? Man-about-town?

"Pardon me, my name is Ranger and I've lost Yogi Bear. I was wondering if you'd see . . ."

"If you watch my suitcases for just five minutes I'll help you look for him."

Her eyes appear to be a very deep blue, and she knows how to play the game.

"What if I steal them?" Still looking helpful I point at her suitcases.

"All forest rangers are honest."

And she vanished toward Pan Am like the indigo lines of the rainbow.

CHAPTER TWO

Higgledy Piggledy Jomo Kenyatta cut up three Britons in the blink of an eye

We are back at the coffee shop, sitting at a booth upholstered in fuchsia-colored imitation leather. Oval coffee in oval cups.

"My name is Carson," I say.

"First or last?"

"Whichever you like. Would you like to think you are calling me by my first or last name?"

"I call my husband by our last name sometimes, if I'm angry or teasing. But you are definitely a first-name person. I'll pronounce Carson like it was your first name."

"And I'll call you Fiona." Quickly I held up my hand to stop the question that was peeking from her lips. The question withdrew, was replaced by another.

"What do you do, Carson?"

"I'll start with something you would believe."

"That would be nice."

"I am a partner in a very successful firm that manufactures aluminum windows. Our head office is in Lexington, Kentucky."

"You're awfully young for the firm to be *very* successful. How old are you?"

"Would thirty be satisfactory?"

"Yes."

"We manufactured our first aluminum window in 1911."

"Which makes part of what you just told me a lie."

"Yes. But which part?"

The waitress brought our toast on a cake plate decorated with a picture of the San Francisco fire.

"Tell me more."

"I'm married. I have a wife named Brady and a daughter who has been eight years old since 1943, simply because I think eight-year-old girls are charming. You'll miss your flight, of course."

I tried to slip the last line in so she wouldn't be surprised, forgetting for the moment that Fiona knew how to play the game.

"I will but I don't know why. No, I take that back, I do, but I could never speak it out loud to anyone."

"There is a very thin line between fantasy and reality. While you were away I drew that line on the airport floor in front of

4

your suitcases. When you stepped over it you became a different person."

"I suppose that's as good an explanation as any. I don't have to stay, do I?"

"Not for a moment longer than you want to. You can still make your flight to Portland. Stay only if you want to forget the reality of planes and schedules and tickets and living fifty more years and becoming a grandmother in Grants Pass, Oregon."

"Did I tell you I was from Grants Pass?"

"No."

"I'm glad," and she half smiled over her coffee, beauty being better uncompleted. "Will it be for long?"

"You know how long you can spend before someone misses you. Can't disrupt your life on the other side of the line. It can be for an hour, a day, the longest was eleven days. Her name was Dierdre. I had to push her back over the line."

"Do you do this often?"

"I've been picking up girls from Grants Pass, Oregon, in the Los Angeles Airport for over eighty years."

"I believe you."

"I'd like very much to touch you, Fiona."

"I think I'd like that too; still it's scary, as though you had some power over me."

"Not over you. Do I look the kind of person who would hurt anyone?"

"No. But all those ladies let the Boston Strangler into their apartments."

"While you make up your mind I'll sit here and look helpful. I want you to notice that when I look helpful, I look a little like a bear, sort of a cross between Yogi and Smokey the . . ."

"I want to touch you too," said Fiona, extending her hands to me across the sleek tabletop.

"On this very spot, as a child, I fell off the back of a giant auk," I said to the cashier as I paid the bill. Fiona giggled prettily.

"Have a nice day," said the cashier.

CHAPTER THREE

Fiona at the Jack and Jill Motel

"Are we real?" asked Fiona.
  "Do you want to be real?"
  "I feel like an apparition."
  "Then so you are."
  "Do apparitions have carnal feelings?"
  "Indeed, they do."
  "I'm glad. I thought for a moment I wasn't normal."

I told Fiona I was a writer, which was a lie. From many years of trial and error I found that girls are not overly impressed by aluminum window salesmen.

Discussing my alleged fictional works I started with a lie the size of an orange, then multiplied my mistakes many fold until the room filled with tricolored beach balls, while I quoted indiscriminately from F. Scott Fitzgerald and Kellogg's Cornflake boxes. Fiona pointed out a cliché that sat huddled in the corner like an eavesdropping cat.

Feeling very worldly, for what could a girl from Grants Pass, Oregon, know about clichés, I said, "Life is a cliché, wrapped in a clear plastic coating. When someone dies I can tell how much he has lived and how close he has come to discovering the truth, by how many pieces of chipped plastic there are in the coffin."

"Then why is the room full of beach balls?"

I launched a new volley of lies, but was suddenly frightened by the sound of a Graf Zeppelin nuzzling the window.

Our lovemaking was not . . . the right word escapes me, certainly not pornographic, which is what I am used to more often than not: a bottle of gin, a motel room, two people far from home, two drinks and drop the laundry. And plastic glasses. There is something deliciously evil about drinking out of plastic glasses. In photocopied motel rooms, love affair after love affair is consummated in the leering presence of vertically

6

furrowed plastic glasses. Should there be reincarnation, I wish to return as one hundred thousand voyeuristic plastic glasses, scattered like tumbleweeds throughout the motel rooms of America.

It was as though we had, perhaps, known each other before. Fiona, soft as foam rubber, smelling of pine soap, her tongue sweet and warm. Neither of us is dissatisfied. I hold her hand and she breathes softly into my shoulder. Could it be that there is something . . .

"Why don't you take off your sock?" asked Fiona sleepily, referring to my nylon-clad right foot.

"I have a cloven hoof," I replied, which was a lie.

"I believe you," said Fiona, which made it true.

In the morning I walked nonchalantly from the shower to the bed.

Fiona was dressing, the odor from deodorants, perfumes and hairsprays filling the room. I draped a sheet around me, then sitting like a San Diego holy man, pretending I was not a liar, took out a pad and paper and began to write.

"How come you never talk to me, Carson?" Fiona said, pronouncing Carson as my last name.

How wonderful that she knew how to play the game.

"Go change a diaper or something," I said without looking up.

"You never talk to me after. All you're interested in is my body." Perfect. Why were so few Fionas? She was sitting in front of the mirror, smoking a cigarette, and putting the finishing touches to her hair. Standing, she put the package of cigarettes in her purse and started for the door.

"Where are you going?"

"To get my hair done."

"You just did your hair."

"Carson, darling, a girl can't go out to get her hair done looking like a slob." She pronounced Carson as my first name.

Fiona had barely closed the door when the phone rang.

7

"Land of the Rising Sun Chastity Belt and Storm Door Company," I said.

"Where the hell have you been?" a nasal voice complained. "I must have phoned twenty hotels until I remembered Carson, you used that once before. Mr. and Mrs. Carson Carson. Don't you have enough imagination to think of two names?"

It was Al my business partner.

"I didn't think you'd find me. There must be thousands of hotels and motels in Los Angeles."

"I know by now I only have to check Orange County. Disneyland has a fatal attraction for you."

"So how is business? Are we selling a lot of whatever it is we sell?"

"Are we selling? For Chrissakes, we got orders falling out the doors. I'm working eighteen hours a day and in the middle of it I have to stop and try to find you."

"A small delay here, Al. I don't want to bother you with details."

"Considerate." The whine in his voice rose an octave or two. "Yes, Mr. Carson, Sir. *Carson*, for Chrissakes. Do you realize I've been looking for you for days?"

"You should have asked Brady. She knows where I am."

"Brady? Who the hell's Brady?"

"My wife."

"Your wife's name isn't . . . and neither is yours."

"Al, I'll be home day after tomorrow, if I don't decide to go to Portland."

"Portland. What the hell do you want to go to Portland for? We're not licensed in Oregon."

"It has to do with my being a forest ranger, Yogi Bear, a library in Grants Pass, Oregon, and a girl named Fiona who has eyes the color of a mauve jelly bean. Does that explain it?"

"All I need, a girl with candy eyes. Does your wife know about her?"

"Who?"

"The jelly bean."

"Of course, I tell Brady everything."

"Brady is not . . . forget it . . . forget Portland. Just get your ass back here. You cost us a fortune every day you're gone."

"Al, you should have been an accountant."

"I am an accountant."

"I knew that there was some reason I went into business with you."

"Just get back here."

"Keep your cool, Al."

"Cool! For Chrissakes."

I hung the telephone up gently. It struck me that everyone has their own particular brand of hell, and, I suppose, for Al, being repeatedly buffaloed by an irresponsible salesman-partner, suffices.

CHAPTER FOUR

Touristy things

Disneyland is the place to be when you're in love. Like love, it is unreal, a mirage in the morning sun, shimmering white like the coats of the attendants with their hippo-mouthed dust-pans, sweeping away imaginary cigarette butts in the ice-cream morning.

The night before Fiona and I talked about love.

"Do you treat every girl you're with as though you're in love with her?"

I looked at her eyes for a long time without replying. The only light in the room was from a far-off neon sign that blinked mildly. The darkness around us was as soft as peach blossoms. I shook my head ever so slightly, still staring into her eyes.

9

"I love you," she said.

"Today," I added. "Always say, today. That way there will never be any promises we can't keep."

"Today," said Fiona. "I love you, today."

Waffles and blueberries, Fiona and raspberry jam, laughing she kissed me across the white wrought-iron table, tasting of June.

Like a doll lifted from Small World, Fiona radiates wonder. Whispers, kisses and hand-clasps, the machinations of new love, her ice-chip laughter cool and exciting as diamonds.

Three times through the Small World, and each time for the tiniest instant, Fiona and I, suspended in plastic reality on the wall among the animated dolls.

"If I hadn't seen it I wouldn't believe it," said Fiona.

"You didn't see it. It was only a wish. Sometimes I can make wishes come true."

"How did you know what I was talking about?"

"Pine trees," I said.

"Pine trees?"

"They put something in your blood that conducts wishes."

A gray-haired matron in a speckled housedress.

"On your honeymoon, I bet."

"Fifth anniversary," says Fiona. We laugh at our wondrous lie, expecting to be inundated by beach balls.

"Where are you from?"

I name a town and plant it in Washington.

"Near Seattle?"

I nod.

"We've cousins in Spokane."

"It's near there too," says Fiona.

"Not possible," says the speckled lady's husband. "They're hundreds of miles apart."

"Anything is possible in Orange County," I say.

The morning is filled with jeweled laughter as we float away, Fiona's arm around my waist and a violet giggle in my shirtsleeve.

"To think I was just going to change planes and go home without ever having seen this," said Fiona staring at the incredible green of the outfield grass under the lights at Angel Stadium.

"It's not that green in Oregon, is it?"

"It's not legal for anything to be that green."

A cranky-looking lady with large tendons in her neck and a very small husband with silver-rimmed glasses occupied the seats in front of us. She drank copious amounts of beer from large, waxy-looking cups. By the fifth inning she was in love with the Angels' first baseman.

"Boy, he can put his shoes under my bed anyday," she said repeatedly for the remainder of the game, glaring around defiantly, wishing, I'm sure, that someone would take exception to her remarks.

"Couldn't you give her her wish," said Fiona.

I tried to look helpful and uncomprehending.

"You intimated that you could do things like that."

"Perhaps just the shoes."

"That's all?"

"It's more than she deserves."

After the ball game we walked twice around the stadium looking for the car I'd rented, and which neither of us had really looked at. Skipping through the acres of growling metal mastiffs, we dodged in and out of traffic lines.

Fiona, arms around my neck, stood on her tiptoes and kissed me in front of a Dodge station wagon full of yelping children, until the driver honked his horn.

"I love you so much I wanted someone else to see, and that car had such soulful headlights."

I lifted her breathless and laughing from in front of the car. We exchanged whispers of "today," and started the search anew.

"James T. Farrell," I said, causing Fiona to stir. She was practically asleep. I lay beside her with a pad and pen, pretending to be what I was not.

"Was he the first baseman?" asked Fiona.

"I read a book of his once, a girl sat in a tree singing 'Blue Ridge Mountains of Virginia.' She was a symbol of springtime. Some men search all their lives for springtime and never find her. Some men have springtime in their arms and let her slip away. That is the way I feel now, Fiona, I don't want to let you slip away."

When I turned to look at her she was asleep.

Dear Fiona, I wrote, you lay, one arm tossed over your head, a velvet smile flickers as you dream your pine-cone dreams. The freckles on your arm seem to blink and rearrange their patterns. We have escaped the oatmeal world, crossed that tingling line between fantasy and reality to a place where we can feel with our hearts. But, for me, time is warped, a splintered bow that wounds the hunter and his game.

You turn in slow motion encircling the pillow with a sigh. Are you back in Grants Pass, Oregon, where I will never be?

I picture your husband in a green checkered mackinaw, smelling of campfires and axe blades. I hope you are friends.

Brady and I were friends, somewhere in the rainbow past. Brady tried to be what I wanted her to be: long-haired girls in blue jeans, high-cheekboned Cherokee girls with dust-colored skin and accusing eyes. And I tried for her, how I tried. Long before James T. Farrell was born . . . I have a daughter who has been eight years old since 1943. Fiona . . . Fiona . . . I wonder if they have a library in Grants Pass, Oregon, and if it has one or two lions guarding the door.

Fiona stirred, woke smiling. "I love you," she said, reluctantly adding, "today." I crumpled the letter and turned out the light.

"Two beaver eggs on toast," I said the next morning at Howard Johnson's. Fiona's eyes full of gentle questions.

"She's been here for sixty years," I said of our stainless-steel waitress. "Not nearly up to my degree though. I got to go home in 1942. Something about war effort.

"By the way, do they have a library in Grants Pass, Oregon?"

"Of course," said Fiona. "I go there every week."

"Does it have a lion?"

"A lion?"

"Guarding the door. All libraries of consequence have lions guarding the door."

"It doesn't even have a beaver. It's part of the consolidated school building."

"No lion," I sighed.

"No lion."

"It should have a lion. It worries me."

"Try not to think about it," said Fiona, her hand exploring mine under the table.

Our waitress hummed into view, bearing beaver eggs, incense and myrrh.

CHAPTER FIVE

Out there

Brady is waiting, in that murky world where twisted time lies tangled like coat hangers on a closet floor. Only I know how long it has been since we have seen each other. Glenn Miller music and patriotism astride the nation like a colossus when we said goodbye.

Brady spins in the tunnel of my life, her eyes veiled membrane, her ears gently filled with cotton. Moving, moving, six months here, a year there. Never more than that for the questions start . . . not questions, comments, that deserve answers. Little jokes like unloaded weapons. "My dear, you don't look a day older than when you came here."

"I swear, Brady dear, that child of yours never grows."

Tic-tac-toe on the face of America. The questions become snub-nosed, steely cold. From Covington, Kentucky, to Bangor, Maine, to Ogden, Utah, they move in Allied Van Lines caravans. That apple-cheeked child, thirty years in the third grade. They are compelled to move, to wait, to be, just as I wait, weekly turning the pages of my notebook for a new name, a new face. An actor with one scene to play, over and over, each time with a new leading lady.

Brady is waiting for my call tonight to tell her I've been delayed. Business is good. I'll be home next week. My two-week business trip stretches into infinity, theirs and mine. The difference is, I know . . . I know.

Somewhere where it is always night, a smiling photo of Brady and myself lies pinioned to a cross of stars, melting away.

CHAPTER SIX

Touristy things: Reprise

Fiona in the rain-fresh morning, her dress, like her eyes, cornflower blue, a wispy scarf in her yellow hair trails after her as she butterflies her way from wonder to wonder.

We are at Knott's Berry Farm. A galaxy of raspberry eyes peer from the plasmatic jam jars that she buys for the folks back home.

The lurch of the train climbing Calico Mountain shifts Fiona's head to my shoulder. She hugs my neck in unrestrained joy, smelling crisp as her new dress.

Tense and wide-eyed Fiona grips my sleeve as the stage is robbed by shirt-tail cousins of mine. White-eyed ghosts of the Youngers and Daltons act out their drama every half hour for eternity, blank guns crackling for a gaggle of slack-jawed tourists. Fiona grips my arm tighter as a black-vested gunfighter dies in the dust at our feet, the cleft in his chin absorbing sunlight.

"It's so exciting. I love it so," she says, seeing only what she was meant to see. Over her shoulder, in the brick-shadowed hills, among tumbleweed, wild onions and whitewashed pools of arsenic water, the Manson women kneel in a covened circle, above a blood-encrusted image, chanting incantations, laughing ingot laughter, beckoning.

Next week, the children of Grants Pass, Oregon, will feast on raspberry jam.

CHAPTER SEVEN

Dr. David Reubens vs. the Outrageous Taco Co.

Night at the Jack and Jill Motel. The pinwheel dreams of satiated tourists flit, batlike, across motel windows. Bluish searchlights illuminate the papier-mâché snow on the Matterhorn peak.

I tipped the delivery boy a dollar, hiding my nakedness by reaching around the edge of the door for the food order.

"I've never done that before," said Fiona.

"Immaculate conception?"

"What?"

"Your children."

"I don't mean *that*. You *know* what I mean."

"You're much more explicit than that when we're making love."

"*You* don't call it making love when we're making love."

"Neither do you."

"I've never done that before either."

"There's a name for it."

"Making love?"

"No. Talking about it."

"Really."

"It's called coprolalia."

"Making love?"

"No. Talking about it."

Tangent sprouts of a visiting nightmare whirl over the pool and courtyard, reflecting eerily on the water and windows.

"There are corn chips on my side of the bed," said Fiona.

CHAPTER EIGHT

The last morning

Seeming to wake at the same time we looked at each other and smiled. Fiona moved as if to get out of bed.

"I want to kiss you very badly," she said, "but common sense tells me I should brush my teeth first." Fiona and my daughter are the only people I know who wake up smiling.

"You've read my thoughts," I said, and moved as if to get up. Fiona lay back on her pillow, her left breast peeking at me over the sheet.

"Me first," I said, swinging my legs over the side. The floor was covered with chips of clear plastic.

At that very moment, a cranky-looking lady in an apartment on Tustin Road, Orange County, California, discovered a pair of size eleven baseball shoes under her bed.

CHAPTER NINE

The man in the glass booth winked at me

At the departure gate the remnants of a charter flight of Portland Viennese jammed the waiting room. We were practically the only ones who spoke English.

A fat, blond boy of five, in leather pants with suspenders, who looked like Hermann Goering, whined into his mother's knee.

Anne Frank sat inconspicuously against the back wall taking notes. I, of course, was the only one who noticed her.

That night, the starboard engine of a Lufthansa jet withered on the tarmac, making Martin Bormann several hours late for dinner.

CHAPTER TEN

The Albert Camus, Western Airlines, Joachin Murieta and Martin Bormann Blues

"I wish you were coming with me."

"No you don't."

"How did you know?"

"Albert Camus said it, 'People say much more than they mean, just for the sake of saying something.' "

"I've never heard of Albert Camus, but whoever he is, he's right."

"If you work it right you can learn how to speak German by the time you get to Portland."

"I virtually never talk to strangers," said Fiona. "Probably one of the children will sit behind me and drop chocolate in my hair."

"See that man over there," I said, pointing to a beagle-eyed gentleman of perhaps sixty, felt hat, green feather, tweed suit, camera on a strap. "He chose the seat next to yours. I suspect he's a college professor. Probably teaches history at a college with lots of green lawns and brick buildings. Start by offering him a cigarette, all college professors like free cigarettes. But don't mention lampshades."

I intended to keep up the pretense right until her plane left, but suddenly it was as if I was encased in cotton batting. We sat silently, too late to speak, we can only touch the moments away.

I mentally composed another letter to Fiona: "Would you like to know the happiest moment I have ever spent at the Los Angeles International Airport? It was when we arrived at the departure gate and the stewardess tried to hand us that mewling Mexican infant wrapped in a blanket the siren pink color of a desert sunset. When we looked blank, she insisted.

" 'He's my baby,' you said, squeezing my arm, your cheek against my shoulder.

"And the stewardess, she had been photographed years before, smiling. Now, each morning, she pastes her photograph over last night's makeup, oils the string on her 'this is a recording' voice and sails off to spend eight hours a day in the Los Angeles International Airport trying to give away Mexican babies to love-sick apparitions.

"Your mauve perfume fills my head, Fiona. I feel . . . spongy, as if I am melting away like ice cream in the sun. How ironic if I should end my days as a neapolitan puddle on the floor of a departure lounge. You bring me back to reality by silently kissing my cheek."

"I suppose I've told you that I'm in partnership in an aluminum window manufacturing plant with an accountant I hate and . . ."

"Camus," Fiona said, touching her finger to my lips.

But, of course, I cannot abide my own advice.

"Fiona, we were meant to be friends, even more than lovers. Delicate magic friends . . ." and on and on I prattled. I used the word magic thirteen times until Fiona finally interrupted me.

"I have no regrets," she said. "What if I didn't want to go back to Grants Pass, and you didn't want to go wherever it is you go?"

I said nothing. I had nearly spoiled it for her.

One more lilac kiss and she was gone. Alone, part of the debris floating on the marble airport sea, I stood. I wandered my domain like a pacing tyrant, trying not to look at my notebook.

I stare at the floor. I wonder how they cut the strange little stones in half? I have tried to count them. My eyes blur in the sepulchral light.

Hours later I phoned the Portland airport and had her paged.

"I wish you hadn't," she said.

"Just wanted to find out if he was a professor."

"He was. He is. Modern European History. Would you like me to say something to you in German?"

"That was all I wanted to know."

"He said something curious, something about teaching for eighty years at the same college."

"I'll write to you."

"Camus," Fiona whispered.

"Of course. I just wanted to hear your voice even if it was only to tell me someone is a professor of European History. I'll send you a lion," I babbled. "Some misty dawn in Grants Pass, Oregon, a lion will mysteriously appear in front of . . . Fiona, I'm not going to hang up. I want to remember you in the tree singing 'Blue Ridge Mountains of Virginia' . . ."

"I love you today," we said together.

In the sagebrush distance, Joachin Murieta rode at full gallop toward the mission of San Luis Obispo, a black sombrero shielding his Aztec eyes, a Mexican baby in each saddlebag.

I left the receiver dangling, spinning slowly like my mind. A trap door seemed to close within me. I stood like a gnarled tree, arms raised, grasping artificial light. Head thrown back, a death rattle in my chest, plastic chips crunching under my shoes, I shrieked the words that had been sealed in my throat all this dusty century.

"Darkness! Deliver me from the Los Angeles International Airport!"

The cashier from the coffee shop looked at me strangely.

A Quite
Incredible
Dance

*M*cArthur felt it was mandatory for a father to dislike his son-in-law, but he had hoped that Gretchen would marry a man he could like. What McArthur had in mind was a big, laughing, easy-going young man, probably an athlete, who would settle comfortably into a public relations career once his playing days were over. He was not insistent, either personally or in his fantasies, that Gretchen marry money. After all, he reflected, about the only advantage having money had afforded him was freedom from having to worry about it.

But instead of fulfilling his fantasy, Gretchen married Vic Vickery. Just hearing about Vic made McArthur's stomach hurt as if it were full of old razor blades and he found himself sitting rigidly, his tongue like a piece of rock pressed against the roof of his mouth, as Gretchen and his wife Marion discussed Vic.

When they finally met, McArthur found Vic even more loathsome than he anticipated. He was short; not only shorter than McArthur, but shorter than Gretchen. He had a wicked-looking Mexican moustache, close-set black eyes that appeared to be all pupil, and glistening black hair in a mod cut that McArthur considered not only too long, but downright sinister. Vic was also a toucher, a man who slapped backs and held your sleeve as he spoke, a practice McArthur despised. He smiled too much and exuded too much energy.

"A hustler if I ever saw one," McArthur intoned to his wife, who countered that Vic was only twenty-four and driving a Cadillac, and reminded McArthur he was thirty before he acquired his first luxury car.

McArthur was inordinately proud of Gretchen. She was his one treasure from a rather pathetic marriage. Marion, after the first good days, had become exactly what society expected of her. She supervised an efficient house, belonged to all the right clubs and charities, even had a half interest in a boutique selling Canadian Indian jewelry. Early on in their relationship she let McArthur know that he was not particularly essential to her well-being.

Gretchen became his ally and confidante, and together they often circumvented Marion's passion for promptness and order. Marion went to the opera. Gretchen, like McArthur, became a baseball fan.

Gretchen clearly resembled her father: she had inherited his lithe good looks and blue-green eyes. Her complexion was clear and her honey-golden hair lay silkily on her shoulders. More important though, she possessed little of her mother's personality. She was neither demanding nor domineering. She woke smiling: some of McArthur's happiest moments during her childhood had been rising early, entering Gretchen's room, and just standing for a moment watching her sleep, her face relaxed, a smattering of freckles across her nose like grains of sand. Then he would touch her shoulder and she would open her eyes, smile and reach out to hug him, smelling of sleep, her arms soft around his neck.

He would open the curtains, patterned with pink and blue ballerinas on a silken material that he and Gretchen had shopped for. Then they would have breakfast together, riotous times, seeing who could dream up and stomach the most outrageous combinations of food. Salmon pancakes, cold Kentucky Fried Chicken with strawberry jam: they shrieked and hugged and splattered batter and crumbs about the kitchen. If Marion joined them, she would sniff with disdain as she drank her black coffee.

McArthur knew that girls often married men who were the exact antithesis of their fathers. But, Vic Vickery for God's sake! Black and white. The princess and the frog. McArthur was desolate, but determined not to alienate Gretchen. He saved his scathing comments like a pile of little hot pokers then scattered them in a shower over Marion the instant Vic left the house. Perhaps left alone and given the opportunity, Vic would destroy his own credibility.

The year Gretchen was twelve she and McArthur traveled a thousand miles to attend two World Series games. Far from Marion and the complex world of stocks and bonds, McArthur felt freer than he ever had before. And Gretchen must have felt it too, for she danced an ingenious, imaginary dance. It was their game. No one else would have understood. Gretchen's imagination was like red ribbons blowing in the wind as she joyously described her prowess as a dancer.

"But, Daddy, I'm so busy and so famous that I spend all my time traveling so I only have time to dance in cars and on trains," said Gretchen, who had never been on a train. "I'm dancing now, Daddy. Won't you dance, too?"

"I would. I should," said McArthur. "We could whirl off across the meadow and up into the hills and not stop until we reached the mountains and not even then if we didn't want to. We could be the most famous dancers in the world, except for one thing," and he pointed down to where his right foot rested on the gas. "This morning I sewed my shoe to the gas pedal. If I dance, I'll have to take the whole car with me. But, perhaps," and he smiled and tapped the dimmer switch a few times with his left foot. Gretchen giggled and launched into a description of how she danced a ballet in full baseball uniform while a covey of outfielders played pepper-ball in the background.

During a quiet time, McArthur suggested that perhaps she would like to take real dancing lessons.

"I only dance for you, Daddy," Gretchen said with her feet flat on the floor. "It's really quite an incredible dance. I could never dance the way I dream, not with a million years of dancing lessons."

They cheered themselves hoarse at the baseball games, not for one team but for the game itself: the ballet of the fielders, the audacity of the runners, the perfection of the game, the strategy, the hits, the magic of hot dogs in the October sun.

They took in all the tourist attractions: Knott's Berry Farm, Marineland of the Pacific, the movie studios. And all the while Gretchen danced: in the car, the tour bus, and even during the helicopter ride from Disneyland to the Los Angeles International Airport. They stayed at a motel near Disneyland where from the window they could see searchlights bathing the Matterhorn peak in bluish light.

"Let's see. You're twelve now. Where do you suppose we'll be ten years from now?" McArthur asked as they breakfasted on strawberry waffles at an ice cream cool concession in Disneyland. The floor was recently hosed white tile, the metal tables white as a movie star's teeth.

"Oh, Daddy, in ten years I'll be married and on my own," said Gretchen. It was perfectly natural for her to assume that in ten years McArthur would no longer be the man in her life, but the realization made a lump form in his throat, although her honesty and simplicity only made him love her more.

They found a restaurant much like one they often visited after baseball games, only more elegant. Chicken Kiev and cheese dumplings served with sour cream came in a dish resembling a blood-colored swan. A Cossack entertainer sang in Russian and danced a wild, heel-clicking dance. Later, a small orchestra played and McArthur urged Gretchen to dance with him. But she was too shy.

They did dance together once, on the way home, in the parking lot of a cool, disinfected motel on the outskirts of San Luis Obispo. McArthur simply grabbed her and whirled her around and they danced across the lot, around and between cars, toward a distant taco stand. And as they danced Gretchen hummed and sang.

"We don't have to stop for walls or streets or freeways or anything, if we don't want to," said Gretchen laughing and breathless, the braces on her teeth glittering golden in the evening sun.

"Only for time," said McArthur, but too softly for her to hear. Out loud he said, "Of course we don't," wishing it were true.

They remained friends, confidantes and baseball fans until Vic Vickery came along. Vic who sold water softeners. H_2O Incorporated was the name of his company. He employed a bevy of ex-alcoholics in shiny suits and suede shoes who slithered from door to door bilking homeowners into buying unneeded water softening devices of some kind.

"I want you to like him, Daddy," Gretchen said, hugging McArthur's neck. Like a villain out of a "B" movie, Vic smoked thin black cigars. McArthur could smell cigar smoke on Gretchen's hair.

"I trust you to make a wise decision," McArthur replied, his stomach burning.

He had Dun and Bradstreet run a check on Vic and was not disappointed with the results: Vic and his company were up to their necks in litigation. It took the Better Business Bureau a half hour just to list last month's complaints about H_2O Inc.

Today, while returning from lunch, McArthur spotted Vic's garish green Cadillac at the curb in front of a restaurant. It was parked in a loading zone and tickets flapped under the windshield wipers. McArthur slammed on his brakes nearly collecting a Datsun on his back bumper as he turned into a parking lot. He entered the restaurant surreptitiously, rather like a spy, he imagined. Shielding his face with a newspaper he had purchased at a coin-box on the street, he peered through the plastic foliage that spiraled up an imitation teakwood divider. For an instant he thought it was Gretchen across the table from Vic. How typical of him to pick a look-alike, and he probably didn't even realize it. The girl was tall, blond, tanned and held tightly to Vic's hand, talking earnestly in his small, ferret face. Vic was smoking one of his little black cigars.

McArthur left as unobtrusively as he had entered, went back across the street to his car and waited. When they came out of the restaurant, he slid down in the seat like a guilty kid, peering at them through the white padded circles of the steering wheel. He need not have bothered. Vic was interested only in the blonde. In order not to lose them, McArthur had to make a left turn from the parking lot. He squealed his tires, cut off a taxi, and forced his way in front of a bus. A very inept way to carry out a surveillance, he thought. Anyone worth his salt would have been a few car lengths behind him instead of across the street. He followed at a discreet distance until they turned into the parking lot of a high rise. He watched the girl unlock the front door, watched Vic's hands brushing her buttocks as he followed her.

At first McArthur considered murder. He would wait for Vic to come out of the building then crush his greasy head with a tire iron. McArthur remembered that he had not actually seen a tire iron for many years, did not own one. There was a time when they were standard equipment with a car. He would shoot him. With some satisfaction, he pictured the surprised look on Vic's face as he emptied a gun methodically into his mid-section. Then McArthur realized somewhat sheepishly that he had never owned or fired a gun. He decided regretfully that he was likely incapable of anything more villainous than a slap in the face or an abortive round-house right. He would rather do nothing than make a fool of himself.

He considered hiring the job done. He had heard that in the skid row area of the city one could hire a murderer, put out a contract it was called, for as little as five hundred dollars. But how would one go about it? He imagined himself walking up to a disreputable-looking young man in an equally disreputable tavern and saying, "Excuse me, but I want someone killed."

McArthur needed time to think. He parked the car and walked into the first bar he came to, a desolate, shabby place that matched his mood.

How could he hurt someone like Vic Vickery? He could run to Gretchen with what he knew, but that would hurt Gretchen, not Vic. Besides, he had vowed never to malign Vic in Gretchen's presence. Perhaps she already knew. She had been less happy than usual recently. She had gained a little weight, let her appearance go a bit, a sure sign, he felt, of marital discord. But until now he had regarded it only as wishful thinking on his part.

The first year of the marriage had been the hardest on McArthur. He virtually never saw Gretchen and when he did, Vic was trailing along like a black cloud that covered the sun. But recently Gretchen had taken to attending ball games with him again. In fact, it was only a week or so ago that, as they were driving home from the ballpark, McArthur had suddenly tapped the dimmer switch a few times, then looked across at Gretchen and they had exchanged happy smiles. She had opened her mouth to speak, perhaps to confide McArthur speculated, then changed her mind.

McArthur knew that if he wanted to, he could ruin Vic financially. Two years ago, just after the marriage, he had considered helping him out for Gretchen's sake. Vic bragged about making two thousand dollars a month, half of which, McArthur surmised, was just that, bragging. Yes, he could bankrupt him; but Vic's kind would just rent another Cadillac, get three more softener units on credit, hire three alcoholics as commission salesmen and be back in business.

Several drinks later, McArthur found his thoughts alternating crazily among Vic Vickery, Disneyland, Gretchen and the blue spruce tree he had planted in his front yard.

The Sunday afternoon after the wedding he and Marion had gone for a drive. McArthur was depressed. His head ached softly and his mouth felt stuffed with flannel. Marion prattled on endlessly about Vic and Gretchen and the honeymoon while McArthur seethed. He could visualize Vic hovering, casting the shadow of a hawk on Gretchen's white body. The thought made McArthur queasy.

Viciously, he told Marion to shut up, then was apologizing before the words were cold. On impulse, he pulled over by a roadside tree nursery and greenhouse. Shady Pine Nursery, the sign read. Trees, their roots turbaned in gunnysack, caught his eye. In a matter of minutes, over Marion's vociferous protests, he had purchased a blue spruce, a white birch and an assortment of begonias and tomato plants.

"You don't garden," Marion kept repeating. "You know Tomas won't allow anyone near the lawn or the garden. It's a pure waste."

"Who owns the house?" McArthur demanded.

"Why, we do, of course."

"Then, if I choose to plant some trees to commemorate my daughter's wedding, I will plant one, or more, and no hired gardener, who can be fired as easily as he was hired, will stop me." McArthur felt quite proud in his assertiveness.

"You do have a hangover, don't you?" said Marion in a saccharine voice.

When they got home McArthur took a shovel and dug a gaping hole in the manicured front lawn and planted the blue spruce about two feet to the right of the sidewalk and about twenty feet from the front of the sprawling ranch house with its green shutters and four-car garage. Marion all the while hovered, complaining. The white birch he planted in the back yard.

"I never realized how sentimental you are," said Marion. "I thought you were unhappy about the marriage," and she stopped to sniff, "I mean, all the uncalled-for things you say about Vic."

"There is nothing sentimental about it," said McArthur, looking Marion straight in the eye. "The tree, my dear, is a symbol. It will grow with the marriage, survive the elements and gardeners like Tomas, just as the marriage will have to survive storms and stresses."

"I suppose it is rather romantic," Marion said. Sometimes McArthur genuinely liked her. She had never been able to tell when she was being put on.

"Don't I look just like Vic," McArthur said, holding one of the smoky-blue fronds beneath his nose.

Marion sniffed. "I think Vic is very handsome," she said. Marion fawned over Vic. In fact McArthur sometimes thought that she acted more like a rival than a mother-in-law. She was forever hugging Vic when she wasn't stuffing him with food that she wouldn't dream of preparing for McArthur when they were alone. In the months preceding the marriage, she and Gretchen had become closer than they had ever been before. Gretchen was not comfortable displaying or discussing her new love in front of McArthur. Something psychological, McArthur assumed. Still he found himself on the outside looking in; Gretchen and Vic and Marion, it seemed, had formed an alliance excluding him.

Just last week on the long drive home from the baseball stadium, Gretchen had fallen asleep. Looking across at her, McArthur noticed the lines around the corners of her mouth. He eased the car to a stop at a traffic light, but the stopping motion jolted Gretchen awake. She smiled and McArthur wanted to comfort her. He wanted her to be a child again, to confide, but he knew better, and only reached across and touched her hand, smiling back.

The bartender informed McArthur that it was closing time.

McArthur swirled the ice in his glass, wondering where the time had gone and hazily weighing the advantages and disadvantages of driving home.

"Would you please call me a taxi?" he said, then laughed into his drink wondering if the bartender might indeed inform him that he was a taxi.

He gave the driver a number two houses from his own. Then, just to be perverse, pretended he was a stranger in the area, and let the driver cruise slowly up and down the street, looking for the number. He wondered vaguely why rich people never put numbers on their houses, or if they did, carefully hid them behind shrubs. When the driver finally found the house, McArthur tipped him extravagantly.

There was a light fog and the cool, sweet air cut into his lungs like the first spray of a cold shower. Walking the half block to his house he stepped carefully and kept his back straight, but his stride was still uneven. "I am walking like a drunk trying to pretend he's sober," McArthur said. He hoped no one was watching. As he swayed up the sidewalk toward the house the outstretched fronds of the blue spruce brushed his ankle.

"You've planted it much too close to the sidewalk," Marion had reminded him when the planting was done. "The roots will break up the sidewalk in a few years and it will have to be cut down."

"The marriage won't last that long," said McArthur, knowing it would get a rise out of Marion.

"Surely you don't intend to get rid of the tree if something happens between Vic and Gretchen," said Marion in an indignant whine, "which it won't if you mind your own business."

"I might," McArthur replied, trying to smile enigmatically. Marion walked away, heels snapping on the cement.

McArthur swayed above the spruce. He gave it a kick and staggered off the sidewalk, almost falling. He grasped the trunk a few inches from the top and pulled up. His hands slipped off and he reeled back, arms spread like bird wings to keep his balance. The needles prickled and his hands were sticky with the clear pungent gum of the tree.

He surveyed the situation. Bending forward from the waist he appeared to seriously study the tree. But for the moment, he was back in that yellow-striped parking lot in San Luis Obispo, and Gretchen, the incredible imaginary dancer, was at his side. He danced a few uncoordinated steps, stopped, and with renewed vigor attacked the tree.

He grasped the trunk firmly and, bracing his feet on the edge of the sidewalk, pulled. His feet slipped and he fell with a thump. The dew-wet grass was cold on his buttocks. The cold seemed to seep up his back and into his head. He began to make sounds somewhere between laughter and sobs as he rose and prepared to assault the tree again. He could hear the calliope-like music of the Disneyland he had shared with Gretchen. The notes seemed to hang in the foggy air. He began to hum. There was, he felt, a terrible irony about his recall of the song, but the significance of it eluded him like a bird fluttering just out of reach.

The tree trunk as he grasped it again was Vic's short, swarthy neck. This time he did not let go. He braced his feet and pulled until the roots began to budge. Then there was a violent release as the roots let go. McArthur found himself flat on his back again, still grasping the tree, covered with clods of dirt. He blinked the damp loam from his eyes, spit the grittiness from his mouth. Standing, he shook the tree like a dog shaking a rat. He wheeled it over his head and was covered in another shower of dirt.

Staggering, he gripped the tree as if he were about to dance a polka with it. Then he began to dance. Slowly, formally, stiffly, his entire body caught up in the music that only he heard. Gradually, the tempo of the music became faster and faster. McArthur danced wildly, wheeling, flying, his feet a blur that carried him across the yard and into the street.

His body became lighter than it ever had been, his feet driven. He made no sound as he danced, no porch lights clicked on, no drapes parted, no one watched. The windows remained pale and blank as he danced with a fervor that no one else saw or knew.

Shoeless
Joe Jackson
Comes to Iowa

*M*y father said he saw him years later playing in a tenth-rate commercial league in a textile town in Carolina, wearing shoes and an assumed name.

"He'd put on fifty pounds and the spring was gone from his step in the outfield, but he could still hit. Oh, how that man could hit. No one has ever been able to hit like Shoeless Joe."

Two years ago at dusk on a spring evening, when the sky was a robin's-egg blue and the wind as soft as a day-old chick, as I was sitting on the verandah of my farm home in eastern Iowa, a voice very clearly said to me, "If you build it, he will come."

The voice was that of a ballpark announcer. As he spoke, I instantly envisioned the finished product I knew I was being asked to conceive. I could see the dark, squarish speakers, like ancient sailors' hats, attached to aluminum-painted light standards that glowed down into a baseball field, my present position being directly behind home plate.

In reality, all anyone else could see out there in front of me was a tattered lawn of mostly dandelions and quack grass that petered out at the edge of a cornfield perhaps fifty yards from the house.

Anyone else was my wife Annie, my daughter Karin, a corn-colored collie named Carmeletia Pope, and a cinnamon and white guinea pig named Junior who ate spaghetti and sang each time the fridge door opened. Karin and the dog were not quite two years old.

"If you build it, he will come," the announcer repeated in scratchy Middle American, as if his voice had been recorded on an old 78-rpm record.

A three-hour lecture or a five-hundred-page guidebook could not have given me clearer directions: dimensions of ball-parks jumped over and around me like fleas, cost figures for light standards and floodlights whirled around my head like the moths that dusted against the porch light above me.

That was all the instruction I ever received: two announce-ments and a vision of a baseball field. I sat on the verandah until the satiny dark was complete. A few curdly clouds striped the moon and it became so silent I could hear my eyes blink.

Our house is one of those massive old farm homes, square as a biscuit box with a sagging verandah on three sides. The floor of the verandah slopes so that marbles, baseballs, tennis balls and ball bearings all accumulate in a corner like a herd of cattle clustered with their backs to a storm. On the north ve-randah is a wooden porch swing where Annie and I sit on hu-mid August nights, sip lemonade from teary glasses, and dream.

When I finally went to bed, and after Annie inched into my arms in that way she has, like a cat that you suddenly find sound asleep in your lap, I told her about the voice and I told her that I knew what it wanted me to do.

33

"Oh love," she said, "if it makes you happy you should do it," and she found my lips with hers, and I shivered involuntarily as her tongue touched mine.

Annie: she has never once called me crazy. Just before I started the first landscape work, as I stood looking out at the lawn and the cornfield wondering how it could look so different in daylight, considering the notion of accepting it all as a dream and abandoning it, Annie appeared at my side and her arm circled my waist. She leaned against me and looked up, cocking her head like one of the red squirrels that scamper along the power lines from the highway to the house. "Do it, love," she said, as I looked down at her, that slip of a girl with hair the color of cayenne pepper and at least a million freckles on her face and arms, that girl who lives in blue jeans and T-shirts and at twenty-four could still pass for sixteen.

I thought back to when I first knew her. I came to Iowa to study. She was the child of my landlady. I heard her one afternoon outside my window as she told her girlfriends, "When I grow up I'm going to marry . . ." and she named me. The others were going to be nurses, teachers, pilots or movie stars, but Annie chose me as her occupation. She was ten. Eight years later we were married. I chose willingly, lovingly to stay in Iowa, eventually rented this farm, bought this farm, operating it one inch from bankruptcy. I don't seem meant to farm, but I want to be close to this precious land, for Annie and me to be able to say, "This is ours."

Now I stand ready to cut into the cornfield, to chisel away a piece of our livelihood to use as dream currency, and Annie says, "Oh, love, if it makes you happy you should do it." I carry her words in the back of my mind, stored the way a maiden aunt might wrap a brooch, a remembrance of a long-lost love. I understand how hard that was for her to say and how it got harder as the project advanced. How she must have told her family not to ask me about the baseball field I was building, because they stared at me dumb-eyed, a row of silent, thick-set peasants with red faces. Not an imagination among them except to forecast the wrath of God that will fall on the heads of pagans such as I.

He, of course, was Shoeless Joe Jackson.

> *Joseph Jefferson (Shoeless Joe) Jackson*
> *Born: Brandon Mills, S.C., July 16, 1887*
> *Died: Greenville, S.C., December 5, 1951*

In April, 1945, Ty Cobb picked Shoeless Joe as the best left fielder of all time.

He never learned to read or write. He created legends with a bat and a glove. He wrote records with base hits, his pen a bat, his book History.

Was it really a voice I heard? Or was it perhaps something inside me making a statement that I did not hear with my ears but with my heart? Why should I want to follow this command? But as I ask, I already know the answer. I count the loves in my life: Annie, Karin, Iowa, Baseball. The great god Baseball.

My birthstone is a diamond. When asked, I say my astrological sign is "hit and run," which draws a lot of blank stares here in Iowa where thirty thousand people go to see the University of Iowa Hawkeyes football team while thirty regulars, including me, watch the baseball team perform.

My father, I've been told, talked baseball statistics to my mother's belly while waiting for me to be born.

My father: born, Glen Ullin, N.D., April 14, 1896. Another diamond birthstone. Never saw a professional baseball game until 1919 when he came back from World War I where he was gassed at Passchendaele. He settled in Chicago where he inhabited a room above a bar across from Comiskey Park and quickly learned to live and die with the White Sox. Died a little when, as prohibitive favorites, they lost the 1919 World Series to Cincinnati, died a lot the next summer when eight members of the team were accused of throwing that World Series.

Before I knew what baseball was, I knew of Connie Mack, John McGraw, Grover Cleveland Alexander, Ty Cobb, Babe

Ruth, Tris Speaker, Tinker-to-Evers-to-Chance, and, of course, Shoeless Joe Jackson. My father loved underdogs, cheered for the Brooklyn Dodgers and the hapless St. Louis Browns, loathed the Yankees, which I believe was an inherited trait, and insisted that Shoeless Joe was innocent, a victim of big business and crooked gamblers.

That first night, immediately after the voice and the vision, I did nothing except sip my lemonade a little faster and rattle the ice cubes in my glass. The vision of the baseball park lingered—swimming, swaying—seeming to be made of red steam, though perhaps it was only the sunset. There was a vision within the vision: one of Shoeless Joe Jackson playing left field. Shoeless Joe Jackson who last played major league baseball in 1920 and was suspended for life, along with seven of his compatriots, by Commissioner Keneshaw Mountain Landis, for his part in throwing the 1919 World Series.

"He hit .375 against the Reds in the 1919 World Series and played errorless ball," my father would say, scratching his head in wonder.

Instead of nursery rhymes, I was raised on the story of the Black Sox Scandal, and instead of Tom Thumb or Rumpelstiltskin, I grew up hearing of the eight disgraced ballplayers: Weaver, Cicotte, Risberg, Felsch, Gandil, Williams, McMullin, and always, Shoeless Joe Jackson.

"Twelve hits in an eight-game series. And *they* suspended *him*," father would cry, and Shoeless Joe became a symbol of the tyranny of the powerful over the powerless. The name Keneshaw Mountain Landis became synonymous with the Devil.

It is more work than you might imagine to build a baseball field. I laid out a whole field, but it was there in spirit only. It was really only left field that concerned me. Home plate was made from pieces of cracked two-by-four embedded in the earth. The pitcher's mound rocked like a cradle when I stood on it. The bases were stray blocks of wood, unanchored. There was no backstop or grandstand, only one shaky bleacher beyond the left-field wall. There was a left-field wall, but only about fifty feet of it, twelve feet high, stained dark green and braced from the rear. And the left-field grass. My intuition told me that it was the grass that was important. It took me three seasons to hone that grass to its proper texture, to its proper color. I made trips to Minneapolis and one or two other cities where the stadiums still have natural grass infields and outfields. I would arrive hours before a game and watch the groundskeepers groom the field like a prize animal, then stay after the game when in the cool of the night the same groundsmen appeared with hoses, hoes, rakes, and patched the grasses like medics attending wounded soldiers.

I pretended to be building a little league ballfield and asked their secrets and sometimes was told. I took interest in their total operation; they wouldn't understand if I told them I was building only a left field.

Three seasons I've spent seeding, watering, fussing, praying, coddling that field like a sick child until it glows parrot-green, cool as mint, soft as moss, lying there like a cashmere blanket. I began watching it in the evenings, sitting on the rickety bleacher just beyond the fence. A bleacher I had constructed for an audience of one.

My father played some baseball, Class B teams in Florida and California. I found his statistics in a dusty minor league record book. In Florida, he played for a team called the Angels and, by his records, was a better-than-average catcher. He claimed to have visited all forty-eight states and every major-league ballpark before, at forty, he married and settled down a two-day drive from the nearest major league team. I tried to play, but ground balls bounced off my chest and fly balls dropped between my hands. I might have been a fair designated hitter, but the rule was too late in coming.

There is the story of the urchin who, tugging at Shoeless Joe Jackson's sleeve as he emerged from a Chicago courthouse, said, "Say it ain't so, Joe."

Jackson's reply reportedly was, "I'm afraid it is, kid."

When he comes, I won't put him on the spot by asking. The less said the better. It is likely that he did accept some money from gamblers. But throw the Series? Never! Shoeless Joe led both teams in hitting in that 1919 Series. It was the circumstances. The circumstances. The players were paid peasant salaries while the owners became rich. The infamous Ten Day Clause, which voided contracts, could end any player's career without compensation, pension, or even a ticket home.

The second spring, on a toothachy May evening, a covering of black clouds lumbered off westward like ghosts of buffalo and the sky became the cold color of a silver coin. The forecast was for frost.

The left-field grass was like green angora, soft as a baby's cheek. In my mind I could see it dull and crisp, bleached by frost, and my chest tightened.

Then I used a trick a groundskeeper in Minneapolis taught me, saying it was taught to him by grape farmers in California. I carried out a hose and making the spray so fine it was scarcely more than fog, I sprayed the soft, shaggy spring grass all that chilled night. My hands ached and my own face became wet and cold, but as I watched, the spray froze on the grass, enclosing each blade in a gossamer-crystal coating of ice. A covering that served like a coat of armor to dispel the real frost that was set like a weasel upon killing in the night. I seemed to stand taller than ever before as the sun rose, turning the ice to eye-dazzling droplets, each a prism, making the field an orgy of rainbows.

Annie and Karin were at breakfast when I came in, the bacon and coffee smells and their laughter pulling me like a magnet.

"Did it work, love?" Annie asked, and I knew she knew by the look on my face that it did. And Karin, clapping her hands and complaining of how cold my face was when she kissed me, loved every second of it.

"And how did he get a name like Shoeless Joe?" I would ask my father, knowing full well the story but wanting to hear it again. And no matter how many times I heard it, I would still picture a lithe ballplayer, his great bare feet, white as baseballs, sinking into the outfield grass as he sprinted for a line drive. Then, after the catch, his toes gripping the grass like claws, he would brace and throw to the infield.

"It wasn't the least bit romantic," my dad would say. "When he was still in the minor leagues he bought a new pair of spikes and they hurt his feet; about the sixth inning he took them off and played the outfield in just his socks. The other players kidded him, called him Shoeless Joe, and the name stuck for all time."

It was hard for me to imagine that a sore-footed young outfielder taking off his shoes one afternoon not long after the turn of the century could generate a legend.

I came to Iowa to study, one of the thousands of faceless students who pass through large universities, but I fell in love with Iowa. Fell in love with the land, the people, with the sky, the cornfields and Annie. Couldn't find work in my field, took what I could get. For years, each morning I bathed and frosted my cheeks with Aqua Velva, donned a three-piece suit and snap-brim hat, and, feeling like Superman emerging from a telephone booth, set forth to save the world from a lack of life insurance. I loathed the job so much that I did it quickly, urgently, almost violently. It was Annie who got me to rent the farm. It was Annie who got me to buy it. I operate it the way a child fits together his first puzzle, awkwardly, slowly, but when a piece slips into the proper slot, with pride and relief and joy.

I built the field and waited, and waited, and waited.

"It will happen, honey," Annie would say when I stood shaking my head at my folly. People look at me. I must have a nickname in town. But I could feel the magic building like a storm gathering. It felt as if small animals were scurrying through my veins. I knew it was going to happen soon.

"There's someone on your lawn," Annie says to me, staring out into the orange-tinted dusk. "I can't see him clearly, but I can tell someone is there." She was quite right, at least about it being *my* lawn, although it is not in the strictest sense of the word a lawn, it is a *left field*.

I watch Annie looking out. She is soft as a butterfly, Annie is, with an evil grin and a tongue that travels at the speed of light. Her jeans are painted to her body and her pointy little nipples poke at the front of a black T-shirt with the single word RAH! emblazoned in waspish yellow capitals. Her red hair is short and curly. She has the green eyes of a cat.

Annie understands, though it is me she understands and not always what is happening. She attends ballgames with me and squeezes my arm when there's a hit, but her heart isn't in it and she would just as soon be at home. She loses interest if the score isn't close or the weather warm, or the pace fast enough. To me it is baseball and that is all that matters. It is the game that is important—the tension, the strategy, the ballet of the fielders, the angle of the bat.

I have been more restless than usual this night. I have sensed the magic drawing closer, hovering somewhere out in the night like a zeppelin, silky and silent, floating like the moon until the time is right.

Annie peeks through the drapes. "There *is* a man out there; I can see his silhouette. He's wearing a baseball uniform, an old-fashioned one."

"It's Shoeless Joe Jackson," I say. My heart sounds like someone flicking a balloon with their index finger.

"Oh," she says. Annie stays very calm in emergencies. She Band-Aids bleeding fingers and toes, and patches the plumbing with gum and good wishes. Staying calm makes her able to live with me. The French have the right words for Annie—she has a good heart.

"Is he the Jackson on TV? The one you yell, 'Drop it, Jackson,' at?"

Annie's sense of baseball history is not highly developed.

"No, that's Reggie. This is Shoeless Joe Jackson. He hasn't played major league baseball since 1920."

"Well, aren't you going to go out and chase him off your lawn, or something?"

Yes. What am I going to do? I wish someone else understood. My daughter has an evil grin and bewitching eyes. She climbs into my lap and watches television baseball with me. There is a magic about her.

"I think I'll go upstairs and read for a while," Annie says. "Why don't you invite Shoeless Jack in for coffee?" I feel the greatest tenderness toward her then, something akin to the rush of love I felt the first time I held my daughter in my arms. Annie senses that magic is about to happen. She knows that she is not part of it. My impulse is to pull her to me as she walks by, the denim of her thighs making a tiny music. But I don't. She will be waiting for me and she will twine her body about me and find my mouth with hers.

As I step out on the verandah, I can hear the steady drone of the crowd, like bees humming on a white afternoon, and the voices of the vendors, like crows cawing.

A little ground mist, like wisps of gauze, snakes in slow circular motions just above the grass.

"The grass is soft as a child's breath," I say to the moonlight. On the porch wall I find the switch, and the single battery of floodlights I have erected behind the left-field fence sputters to life. "I've shaved it like a golf green, tended it like I would my own baby. It has been powdered and lotioned and loved. It is ready."

Moonlight butters the whole Iowa night. Clover and corn smells are thick as syrup. I experience a tingling like the tiniest of electric wires touching the back of my neck, sending warm sensations through me like the feeling of love. Then, as the lights flare, a scar against the blue-black sky, I see Shoeless Joe Jackson standing out in left field. His feet spread wide, body bent forward from the waist, hands on hips, he waits. There is the sharp crack of the bat and Shoeless Joe drifts effortlessly a few steps to his left, raises his right hand to signal for the ball, camps under it for a second or two, catches the ball, at the

41

same time transferring it to his throwing hand, and fires it into the infield.

I make my way to left field, walking in the darkness far outside the third-base line, behind where the third-base stands would be. I climb up on the wobbly bleacher behind the fence. I can look right down on Shoeless Joe. He fields a single on one hop and pegs the ball to third.

"How does it play?" I holler down.

"The ball bounces true," he replies.

"I know." I am smiling with pride and my heart thumps mightily against my ribs. "I've hit a thousand line drives and as many grounders. It's true as a felt-top table."

"It is," says Shoeless Joe. "It is true."

I lean back and watch the game. From where I sit the scene is as complete as in any of the major league baseball parks I have ever attended: the two teams, the stands, the fans, the lights, the vendors, the scoreboard. The only difference is that I sit alone in the left-field bleacher and the only player who seems to have substance is Shoeless Joe Jackson. When Joe's team is at bat, the left fielder below me is transparent as if he were made of vapor. He performs mechanically, but seems not to have facial features. We do not converse.

A great amphitheater of grandstand looms dark against the sky, the park is surrounded by decks of floodlights making it brighter than day, the crowd buzzes, the vendors hawk their wares, and I cannot keep the promise I made myself not to ask Shoeless Joe Jackson about his suspension and what it means to him.

While the pitcher warms up for the third inning we talk.

"It must have been . . . It must have been like . . ." but I can't find the words.

"Like having a part of me amputated, slick and smooth and painless, like having an arm or a leg taken off with one swipe of a scalpel, big and blue as a sword," and Joe looks up at me and his dark eyes seem about to burst with the pain of it. "A friend of mine used to tell about the war, how him and a buddy was running across a field when a piece of shrapnel took his friend's head off, and how the friend ran, headless, for several strides before he fell. I'm told that old men wake in the night and scratch itchy legs that have been dust for fifty years. That was me. Years and years later, I'd wake in the night with the smell of the ballpark in my nostrils and the cool of the grass on my feet. The thrill of the grass . . ."

How I wish my father could be here with me. He died before we had television in our part of the country. The very next year he could have watched in grainy black and white as Don Larsen pitched a no-hitter in the World Series. He would have loved hating the Yankees as they won that game. We were always going to go to a major league baseball game, he and I. But the time was never right, the money always needed for something else. One of the last days of his life, late in the night while I sat with him because the pain wouldn't let him sleep, the radio dragged in a staticky station broadcasting a White Sox game. We hunched over the radio and cheered them on, but they lost. Dad told the story of the Black Sox Scandal for the last time. Told of seeing two of those World Series games, told of the way Shoeless Joe Jackson hit, told the dimensions of Comiskey Park, and how during the series the mobsters in striped suits sat in the box seats with their colorful women, watching the game and perhaps making plans to go out later and kill a rival.

"You must go," he said. "I've been in all sixteen major league parks. I want you to do it too. The summers belong to somebody else now, have for a long time." I nodded agreement.

"Hell, you know what I mean," he said, shaking his head. I did indeed.

"I loved the game," Shoeless Joe went on. "I'd have played for food money. I'd have played free and worked for food. It was the game, the parks, the smells, the sounds. Have you ever held a bat or a baseball to your face? The varnish, the leather. And it was the crowd, the excitement of them rising as one when the ball was hit deep. The sound was like a chorus. Then there was the chug-a-lug of the tin lizzies in the parking lots and the hotels with their brass spittoons in the lobbies and brass beds in the rooms. It makes me tingle all over like a kid on his way to his first doubleheader, just to talk about it."

The year after Annie and I were married, the year we first rented this farm, I dug Annie's garden for her; dug it by hand, stepping a spade into the soft black soil, ruining my salesman's hands. After I finished it rained, an Iowa spring rain as soft as spray from a warm hose. The clods of earth I had dug seemed to melt until the garden leveled out, looking like a patch of black ocean. It was near noon on a gentle Sunday when I walked out to that garden. The soil was soft and my shoes disappeared as I plodded until I was near the center. There I knelt, the soil cool on my knees. I looked up at the low gray sky; the rain had stopped and the only sound was the surrounding trees dripping fragrantly. Suddenly I thrust my hands wrist-deep into the snuffy-black earth. The air was pure. All around me the clean smell of earth and water. Keeping my hands buried I stirred the earth with my fingers and I knew I loved Iowa as much as a man could love a piece of earth.

When I came back to the house Annie stopped me at the door, made me wait on the verandah, then hosed me down as if I were a door with too many handprints on it, while I tried to explain my epiphany. It is very difficult to describe an experience of religious significance while you are being sprayed with a garden hose by a laughing, loving woman.

"What happened to the sun?" Shoeless Joe says to me, waving his hand toward the banks of floodlights that surround the park.

"Only stadium in the big leagues that doesn't have them is Wrigley Field," I say. "The owners found that more people could attend night games. They even play the World Series at night now."

Joe purses his lips, considering.

"It's harder to see the ball, especially at the plate."

"When there are breaks they usually go against the ball-players, right? But I notice you're three for three so far," I add, looking down at his uniform, the only identifying marks a large S with an O in the top crook, an X in the bottom, and an American flag with forty-eight stars on his left sleeve near the elbow.

Joe grins. "I'd play for the Devil's own team just for the touch of a baseball. Hell, I'd play in the dark if I had to."

I want to ask about that day in December, 1951. If he'd lasted another few years things might have been different. There was a move afoot to have his record cleared, but it died with him. I wanted to ask, but my instinct told me not to. There are things it is better not to know.

It is one of those nights when the sky is close enough to touch, so close that looking up is like seeing my own eyes reflected in a rain barrel. I sit in the bleacher just outside the left-field fence. I clutch in my hand a hot dog with mustard, onions and green relish. The voice of the crowd roars in my ears like the sea. Chords of "The Star-spangled Banner" and "Take Me Out to the Ballgame" float across the field. A Coke bottle is propped against my thigh, squat, greenish, the ice-cream-haired elf grinning conspiratorially from the cap.

Below me in left field, Shoeless Joe Jackson glides over the plush velvet grass, silent as a jungle cat. He prowls and paces, crouches ready to spring as, nearly three hundred feet away, the ball is pitched. At the sound of the bat he wafts in whatever direction is required as if he were on ball bearings.

Then the intrusive sound of a screen door slamming reaches me, and I blink and start. I recognize it as the sound of the door to my house and looking into the distance, I can see a shape that I know is my daughter toddling down the back steps. Perhaps the lights or the crowd has awakened her and she has somehow eluded Annie. I judge the distance to the steps. I am just to the inside of the foul pole, which is exactly 330 feet from home plate. I tense. Karin will surely be drawn to the lights and the emerald dazzle of the infield. If she touches anything, I fear it will all disappear, perhaps forever. Then as if she senses my discomfort she stumbles away from the lights, walking in the ragged fringe of darkness well outside the third-base line. She trails a blanket behind her, one tiny fist rubbing a sleepy eye. She is barefoot and wears a white flannelette nightgown covered in an explosion of daisies.

She climbs up the bleacher, alternating a knee and a foot on each step, and crawls into my lap, silently, like a kitten. I hold her close and wrap the blanket around her feet. The play goes on; her innocence has not disturbed the balance.

"What is it?" she says shyly, her eyes indicating that she means all that she sees.

"Just watch the left fielder," I say. "He'll tell you all you ever need to know about a baseball game. Watch his feet as the pitcher accepts the sign and gets ready to pitch. A good left fielder knows what pitch is coming and he can tell from the angle of the bat where the ball is going to be hit and, if he's good, how hard."

I look down at Karin. She cocks one sky-blue eye at me, wrinkling her nose, then snuggles into my chest, the index finger of her right hand tracing tiny circles around her nose.

The crack of the bat is sharp as the yelp of a kicked cur. Shoeless Joe whirls, takes five loping strides directly toward us, turns again, reaches up, and the ball smacks into his glove. The final batter dawdles in the on-deck circle.

"Can I come back again?" Joe asks.

"I built this left field for you. It's yours any time you want to use it. They play 162 games a season now."

"There are others," he says. "If you were to finish the infield, why, old Chick Gandil could play first base, and we'd have the Swede at shortstop and Buck Weaver at third." I can feel his excitement rising. "We could stick McMullin in at second, and Cicotte and Lefty Williams would like to pitch again. Do you think you could finish the center field? It would mean a lot to Happy Felsch."

"Consider it done," I say, hardly thinking of the time, the money, the backbreaking labor it entails. "Consider it done," I say again, then stop suddenly as an idea creeps into my brain like a runner inching off first base.

"I know a catcher," I say. "He never made the majors, but in his prime he was good. Really good. Played Class B ball in Florida and California . . ."

"We could give him a try," says Shoeless Joe. "You give us a place to play and we'll look at your catcher."

I swear the stars have moved in close enough to eavesdrop as I sit in this single rickety bleacher that I built with my un-skilled hands, looking down at Shoeless Joe Jackson. A breath of clover travels on the summer wind. Behind me, just yards away, brook water plashes softly in the darkness, a frog shrills, fireflies dazzle the night like red pepper. A petal falls.

"God, what an outfield," he says. "What a left field." He looks up at me and I look down at him. "This must be heaven," he says.

"No. It's Iowa," I reply automatically. But then I feel the night rubbing softly against my face like cherry blossoms; look at the sleeping girl-child in my arms, her small hand curled around one of my fingers; think of the fierce warmth of the woman waiting for me in the house; inhale the fresh-cut grass smell that seems locked in the air like permanent incense, and listen to the drone of the crowd, as below me Shoeless Joe Jackson tenses, watching the angle of the distant bat for a clue as to where the ball will be hit.

"I think you're right, Joe," I say, but softly enough not to disturb his concentration.

Waiting
for the
Call

*P*op died in January. No
insurance. No savings. He
was an amiable man. I think he and Mother were happy. I probably would have noticed if they weren't.

Mother, in spite of being over forty, got a job as a clerk with
the telephone company. We moved from a rather comfortable
apartment to this house on Manitoba Street. Out of the high
rent district. Warehouses abound. The car barns behind us, a
concrete block manufacturing plant behind the houses across
the street. To those outside, Manitoba Street is known as The
Pit. I don't think we really had to move, but Mother wanted
to prove to the world that she could take care of her family. I
think she had secretly been looking forward to widowhood.

Our landlord, a gypsy capable of putting a curse on your
house, rented with the agreement that the first two years' rent
could be applied as a down payment. Verbal only. Good for an
extra ten dollars per month on the rent.

"Mom," I said, "I'm through school. I'll be getting that full-time job soon. I'm the man of the house now. I'll look after you and Julie."

"Don't be ridiculous, Tipton. What would happen in a year or two when you want to start a life of your own?"

Case closed. One does not argue with my mother. Incidentally, Tipton was my mother's maiden name.

I am waiting for a call to go to work on a weather ship. I graduated from high school in June with 90% in English, 51% in each of seven other subjects, the nature of which I have already forgotten. I think I would like to be a writer. Mother arranged with a friend of Pop's to get me on the waiting list for the weather ships.

In the meantime, I box chicken and sweep floors three nights a week at Big Al's Chicken Shack. Big Al looks like a retired middleweight, smokes cigars, drives a Cadillac, has a dumpy little Italian wife who makes coleslaw and a girlfriend named Lulu who looks the part.

The Pit. The only unpaved street in the entire city. Every time the city fathers consider paving, the gypsy forces his tenants to sign a petition opposing it. Manitoba Street is only one block long.

The houses are identical. Four on each side of the street. Tall, sad, two-storey, frame, peeling paint, listing porches, look like miniature grain elevators with windows.

To the right, Mr. Gorman Tailfeathers, his wife, seven children, several of whom have husbands, wives, paramours, children, legitimate and otherwise, of their own. Several aunts, uncles, cousins, everyone with Indian blood qualifies as a cousin, and a grandmother who walks with a cane, wears a dress the same color as the scrawny Plymouth Rocks that scratch furtively in the garbage, chatters in Cree and points an accusing arthritic finger at anyone who comes within range of her limited vision. Tailfeathers' yard is crammed with wrecked cars, washing machines and bedsprings. The quack grass is waist high, the sow thistle even higher and in bloom.

On the left, Bev and Sammy. Bev was born a broad. She is the kind of a broad whose ambition in life is to be a broad, therefore she has never had anything to strive for. She is twenty-three, five up on me. Wide, placid face with pale corn-flaky freckles, mild blue eyes, heavy white arms and legs, partial to short skirts and tight sweaters. Has two dirty little children of indeterminate sex whom she ignores.

Sammy wears a charcoal suit, pink shirt, narrow black tie. Is of the opinion that he is ultra-cool. Suit has a cigarette burn at the knee. Hustles pool, collects welfare, occasionally hustles Bev, usually to pay off gambling debts. He is about thirty, thin, hatchet features, oiled hair. Missing teeth lower right, upper left, remaining teeth and index fingers identical tobacco color. Speaks in a soft whine to everyone but Bev whom he curses at loudly. Travels by taxi, leaves midafternoon, comes home after midnight. When phone is cut off for nonpayment, which is most of the time, sends Bev to our place to phone his taxi for him.

The gypsy. The eight houses on Manitoba Street and several others in the general area are owned by one Muftafa Baldararian, rug dealer, corpulent, thick-lipped and gold-toothed, wears a watch chain, probably has a watch on it. Has a passion for young girls. Collects the rent in person, drooling. My sister, Julie, is fourteen.

My sister. Julie is a snitch, has pimples, freckles, big teeth, a shrill voice, five hundred movie magazines. Favorite word is pervert. Baldararian is welcome to her.

Next to Bev and Sammy are the Italians. Four, five, perhaps six families, stacked like cases of cooking oil. Several of them own gravel trucks which are parked up and down both sides of the narrow street, differentials dripping in the dirt. Tidy people. Lace curtains on the windows. Short, swarthy, barrel-chested men dig in the yard in the evenings. They grow broad beans, green melons in obscene shapes, pinto beans and many small dark-eyed children.

Upstairs at the Italians, Guillamino Vasquez y Garcia. Portuguese. Recently evicted by a mental hospital. Hollow chested, looks at the ground with small wet eyes. Used to work as a busboy. Ambition is to open a restaurant specializing in curried chicken à la king. Cooks chicken à la king on the hot-plate in his attic. Unable to comprehend that no one appears to buy it. Shyly, he gives the food to the hippies across the street. In appreciation, they give him a few marijuana plants from their garden. He boils and eats them like spinach.

Ramona Black-eye. Claims to be the daughter of Gorman Tailfeathers' son-in-law's sister. Good enough to get her free room and board. Wears faded blue jeans with no belt. T-shirt with red lettering says, Custer Had It Coming. No bra. Titties point up. Belly button shows between jeans and T-shirt. Ramona is full-lipped, salmon-colored, no inhibitions, laughs easily and genuinely. Calls me white trash. Wears a pair of scuffed calf-high boots. Tucks jeans inside. I have an erection whenever I am with her. Have been reading about fetishes in *A Thousand Tongues and Other Stories,* a very well written porno book that I keep secreted between my mattress and box spring.

The hippies. Mundane. An equal number of dogs and humans. A dune-buggy painted with sunflowers, driven by a troll-like creature who thinks he is Charles Manson. Most of his dogs are better looking than most of his girls.

Next to them a battalion of Pakistanis darken the windows. Reeking of curry, turbaned, smiling obsequiously, they babble in chicken tracks. Two of them own taxis which they drive into each other trying to get in and out of the driveway.

I have few friends. Uncomfortable with men. Only slightly less uncomfortable with women. One connection with the past is Cassie Bednarsky, the sometime love of my life. Cassie has dark hair, delicate features, one gold inlay, tiny little hands like a child.

Cassie lives in our old neighborhood. I have to bus four miles to see her, leave before 11:30 to catch the last bus back. Her father never leaves the living room, reads a Ukrainian newspaper full of upside-down writing. Her mother wears a babushka, cooks beets twenty-four hours a day. Cassie lets me take off her bra.

We walk to the playground. Stand in the shadow of the equipment shack, smoke cigarettes, French kiss. Wonder what we'll do when winter comes. Bra sticks. Hooks definitely welded together. Pull it down. Hangs on her hips. Suggest we try some pleasures I have read about in *A Thousand Tongues and Other Stories*. Brought the book with me one time, Cassie wouldn't even look at the pictures.

Cassie: "I don't do none of that vomity stuff."

Case closed. I help her pull up her bra.

Next to the Pakistanis, a welfare mom with many children. Wears a stained red cloth coat with the lining hanging down. Followed everywhere by a row of snotty noses. Goes to the Canadian Legion on Saturday nights, picks up losers who, somewhere, have abandoned families just like hers. Even dressed up there is a faint smell of diapers about her. Respectability is terribly important. She is the kind of dismal woman who gets balled standing up in the front hall because the children might wake up.

Baldararian advertises under Houses for Rent, hippies and welfare mothers welcome. When the hippies can't pay he takes the rent out in trade with the denimed, bra-less girls who loll, smoking, on the decomposing front steps.

Midnight. Bring Ramona to my room. Much tiptoeing. Goddamned bed squeaks. How was I to know?

Julie: "How much is it worth not to tell Ma?"

Four dollars for a Bruce Lee poster. A bucket of chicken for her and her pussy friends on Saturday night. The use of my record player.

She tells Mother on Sunday. I endure a two-hour lecture on the evils of Indians and immorality. Disregard a suggestion that I visit the VD Clinic. Mother washes my clothes separately from hers and Julie's.

Postman arrives at hippie house with package, considerable postage due. Troll anxious to claim it, probably contains dope from comrades south of the border. Frantic search produces no money. Troll commands one of his girls to perform what many would consider a perverted sex act on postman in lieu of postage due. Postman, an elderly Scot whose standard greeting to everyone is "Lousy weather," flees in panic, sans package. Will no doubt regale fellow workers with variously lewd versions of the incident until retirement.

Bought a spring mousetrap. Set it under back porch. Caught three in an hour. Took them to work wrapped in newspaper. Toward end of evening, batter and deep-fry, mix with order of prawns. Surprise for snitch sister.

Big Al sells order to customer while I am in john. Panic. Picture being interrogated by Board of Health, Chief of Police, unsympathetic judge with rodent face. Sweat constantly for forty-eight hours. No complaints. Wonder who ate them?

The houses are only about four feet apart. My room is opposite Bev and Sammy's. All windows are open during humid summer and fall. I lie awake listening for sound of taxi wheels on gravel. Sammy slams front door, thumps around house for a while, finally goes to bedroom. Calls Bev out for the filthy house and kids and for having no food or liquor. Runs through a remarkably complete repertory of profanity. Bev whines a lot, tells him how much she loves him. He beats on her for a while. They fuck. Lots of noise and loud bodily contact. Sammy is a jackhammer fucker.

The Coffin Chasers: their front porch sags under the weight of several hundred dozen empty beer bottles. Furniture consists of several mattresses, three fridges full of beer.

They take their chromed beauties into the house, into their beds too, I suppose. There are six guys, two bedraggled girls. Early evening they line up in ragged formation, choppers growling like leashed mastiffs. Hours later they return in ones and twos, heads bandaged, colors mutilated. Their leader is bareheaded, someone has stolen his Nazi helmet. As a gang they strike fear into the hearts of very few.

Occasionally, one staggers from the house, passes out in the tiny front yard. Tailfeathers' chickens peck respectfully around him until he revives.

Rumor has it that to initiate a new member, each Coffin Chaser drinks a dozen bottles of beer without benefit of a potty break. They then, simultaneously, piss on the new member, who must wear his clothes for six consecutive months without washing, or until they rot off, whichever comes first. To the best of my knowledge the rumor has no basis in fact.

Drag an old mattress under Tailfeathers' back steps. There is warmth wherever Ramona and I may be.

Julie discovered us. Sits cross-legged on a chair chanting pervert, as Mother lectures. When Mother is angry there is a definite Scots burr to her words. Do I want a fat, drunken Indian wife with a mob of half-breed children? I try to look repentant, planning revenge on Julie. May shave her head, donate her to Hare Krishnas who chant on street corners. Hare Krishna! Hare Rama! Pervert! Pervert!

Early evening. A herd of police cars converges on a house across the street. They are raiding the hippies for dope. They charge the door of the Pakistani house. The door splinters. They enter, only to be driven back by clouds of curry. Next door the john flushes, groaning like a prehistoric beast.

The next afternoon the same officers who smashed the door, under Baldararian's slug-lipped gaze, replace it with a new one. Baldararian has friends in high places.

I coffee with Bev in the afternoons. Sometimes I have to bring the coffee. Bev smokes my cigarettes. Her kids eat crackers, heavy diapers sag around their knees. When Bev does get money she buys Sara Lee frozen cake, expensive cheese, or sends out for Chinese food.

Today, she fingers her little purple disc of birth control pills.

"I can never remember when to take these damn things."

"You just take one a day."

"Yeah, but I always forget."

"It's got the date right beside each pill."

"I don't have a calendar so I never know what day it is."

"You'll be sorry if you get knocked up again."

"Aw, I don't suppose one more would make any difference to me."

"Why don't you just take one before you go to bed?"

"I go to bed at different times."

Convinced, I change the subject.

Cree grandmother in back yard among ruins. Bent, black-shawled, like a crow walking away. Points arthritic finger at me and cackles. Ramona appears.

"Tell her I'm going to sacrifice a dog to the Great Spirit in Sammy's yard at midnight and that she's welcome to attend."

Much palaver.

Ramona smiles, breaks down in laughter.

"Grandmother says you're full of shit."

Ramona. Everything I suggest to Ramona she agrees to. Says she's done it before. Oiled bedsprings. Braced steep steps to my room. Ramona visits almost every night. Think I am in love. Haven't been to see Cassie for three weeks, may not go for another three. Have exhausted all eleven chapters of *A Thousand Tongues and Other Stories*. Plan to plant book in Julie's room where Mother will find it.

Making coffee in Bev's kitchen, I slip my arms around her waist from the back, place one hand up under her sweater. She pulls away quickly, crosses room.

"Hey, I'm married, you know. I don't fool around on my old man."

I am standing with my back to her. Take a deep breath. Have decided to pull a Sammy. "Well, you're gonna fool around today, 'cause I tell you to. We're going up to the bedroom and I'm gonna beat the piss out of you if you don't do exactly as I say."

55

All is lost. My voice broke on the word piss. I peek over my shoulder for Bev's reaction.

She is already unbuttoning her skirt and looking at me with adoration.

My presence requested at the home of Gorman Tailfeathers. Twenty Indians and me sit in sparse living room. Very little English spoken. Ramona has taught me to swear in Cree. I am able to understand quite a bit of what is being said. Ramona smokes prettily, flicks ashes behind chesterfield.

Relative of some kind wearing headband, fluorescent orange shirt: "We don't like white men who mess around with our women."

Plain enough. He looks like a photograph of Cochise. Grandmother cackles. Wonder how long since a white man walked the gauntlet? Judge distance to door. Multiply by number of Indians. Unrealistic total.

Decide to bluff it out. I tell them I love Ramona. Add truly for good measure. Forty black eyes wet me down. I tell them of my upcoming job. Several dark heads together translating monthly income into dozens. Progress.

Ramona winks at me. Feel relief.

Gorman Tailfeathers is not the head of this clan for nothing. He counts last coup. He pronounces a magic number that paralyzes my law-abiding heart. Ramona is only fifteen.

"Jail bait," screeches Cree grandmother, slapping her cane on the metal space heater.

Ramona in my room an hour later: "Screw them all, I ain't no teepee squaw."

A week later: tragedy. Ramona is gone. No one at Tailfeathers' speaks English anymore. Two long days before one of the children talks to me.

Her man came for her, some dude who was working in the bush for the summer. She put up a ruckus but a couple of cousins helped out. They are vague, name locations from one end of the province to the other, where Ramona may have gone. Choice is between suicide and Cassie Bednarsky. Will have to consider carefully.

Cassie's parents actually leave their house. Niece being married. Seven-day orgy of potato dumplings and sour cream being planned in her honor.

Take off Cassie's bra, skirt, sweater, panties, socks. Bedroom is cold. Bed covered in frigid purple spread. Garish picture of the Virgin watches with a baleful eye.

Cassie cries. I tell her I love her. We eat potato chips, drink 7-Up, watch TV afterward. She kisses me goodnight with salty lips. I have never felt so sad.

December 24. My mother, who should know better, says something about those less fortunate, goes over and lays twenty dollars on Bev, after Sammy has departed, so she can buy presents for kids, maybe have a Christmas dinner.

Bev takes the bus uptown. Returns in a taxi with the largest gift-wrapped package I have ever seen. No toys. No food. Explains the present is for Sammy.

Christmas morning. Sammy throws the half-unwrapped Christmas present out the back window of their house. It is long and lean and sticks in the snow like a spear from another planet. Peeking from the dull brown-and-green Christmas wrapping, featuring scenes of the crucifixion, is a shiny red-and-white metal stepladder. To the mystification of Mother and Julie, I laugh myself senseless.

I coffee with Bev the next day.

The kitchen window is bandaged amateurishly with cardboard and electric tape.

"Sammy didn't like his present" is all she says, smiling sadly, her eyes full of incomprehension.

That night I sleep poorly, alternately dozing and staring at the frost patterns on the window.

I would like to belong. Anywhere. I don't belong with Mother and Julie, though their genes rattle around in me. What I want beyond acceptance is as much a mystery to me as the artistry of the snowscapes on the window. I wish I could walk into the hippies' house, sit at their crusted kitchen table and just pass the time. Instead of eyeing me suspiciously when I walk by I wish the young gargoyle would say to me, "Come in, Brother," as he does to other unkempt types who wander down into The Pit.

And the Coffin Chasers. To walk across a roomful of them and see no curiosity in their eyes is something I know I will never experience. I understand their loyalty, so why can't I belong? I'd walk through a wall for one icy-eyed nod of acceptance from the most disreputable of them.

And Ramona. If only I knew where to look, I'd settle for her. Going God knows where together. I need her shy sureness, her warm body, her biting kisses, nails tearing at my shoulders.

But I see myself married to Cassie Bednarsky. Cassie who sleeps in flannel pajamas. Eight rooms of furniture in a four-room house. Children with tiny little hands. Visiting Cassie's parents on Sunday. Mother and Julie dropping by dressed in paisley slip covers. The smell of caraway, the odor of cooking beets.

"I don't do none of that vomity stuff."

I wait. Stuffing buckets with chicken I wait for the call, wait for the opportunity to sit for ninety days off the coast in the fog. All my life I've been absorbing bits of the people around me. Now, in a great dream-vision, all that I've stored up pours out of my fingertips like steaming streams of blood onto paper. It is almost morning. My stomach hurts.

December 28. My call came today. I am to report for work at midnight on a weather ship called the *Marmalade*.

Mother wraps an extra scarf around my neck, makes me promise to change my underwear, be careful crossing streets, and not grow a beard.

After much urging from Mother, Julie agrees to kiss me goodbye. We embrace for Mother's benefit and whisper to each other.

Julie: "Indian fucker."

Me: "I hope you get syphilis."

As I tramp down the rickety back steps the snow squeaks under my feet. The sky is clear and there is a bright moon.

The stepladder lies at an eerie angle in the snow like a drunk pitched on his head. I look at it. Sammy threw it through the window. The Indians would put it out with the bedsprings and wrecked cars. The Italians would sell it to an auction and use the money for garden seeds. Guillamino Vasquez y Garcia would talk to it. The hippies would refuse to own it. The Coffin Chasers would break it. The Pakistanis wouldn't understand the mechanical principle of it. What about me?

Setting down my duffle bag I plod across the yard, snow filling my shoes. I hoist the ladder on my left shoulder like a frozen corpse and start off across the town. Instead of going to the harbor and my rendezvous with the *Marmalade*, I head for the bus depot.

I present the stepladder to a bewildered wino in front of the bus depot and buy a ticket to the first of many places where Ramona may be. I have $8.14 in my pockets, but the climb has done me good. There are several thousand dollars worth of adrenaline coursing through my body.

Sister Ann
of the
Cornfields

Sister Ann appeared in a cornfield, behind three strands
of barbed-wire fence, alongside a lightly used secondary highway in the state of Iowa.

Sister Ann waved in benediction to each passing vehicle.
They were mainly farm pickups, tractors and teenage boys in
hotrods. Sister Ann wore a flowing white robe tied at the
waist with an ice-blue ribbon. Her hair flowed to her shoulders, the burnished tone of sunflowers. Her robe was soft and
loose; it brushed against the tops of her bare feet which were
firmly planted in the dark soil. Listening to the greenness of
the corn Sister Ann shivered in the soft Iowa dusk.

"The sky is my tabernacle," Sister Ann said to the first
farmer who stopped his pickup and idly looked at her. The
farmer cleared his throat and spat on the highway.

"I'll be damned," he said.

"Perhaps, perhaps not," replied Sister Ann.

A few days later a truck driver stopped his flatbed, got out and walked over to lean on the fence and look at Sister Ann. She smiled and waved her fingers at him.

"You look hot out there, lady. Would you like a beer?"

"Christ died for your sins," said Sister Ann. Rain had sketched patterns, delicate as black lace, on her bare feet and the hem of her gown.

"You want a beer or not," said the truck driver.

"Pour it at my feet."

"The hell! Beer costs good money."

"Wilt thou that we command fire to come down from heaven?" asked Sister Ann demurely. "Luke 9:54."

"In town they say you're crazy."

"Pour it at my feet," said Sister Ann, and the sky appeared to darken, although it was cloudless and noon.

The driver poured three-quarters of a can of Pabst Blue Ribbon on the ground just over the fence.

"Bless you," said Sister Ann, digging her toes into the cool soil.

The next day the owner of the property appeared.

"What are you doing out here, Miss?"

"I am waiting for a miracle."

"Yeah? Well, you notice the corn ain't growing the way it should around where you're standing. I could charge you rent, you know." He was a red-faced farmer in bib overalls. His right cheek bulged with a cud of snuff.

"The meek shall inherit, etcetera," said Sister Ann.

"Etcetera?" said the farmer, who had not shaved that day.

"You know the quotation. There's no need for me to finish it."

"Makes sense," said the farmer. "You from around here?"

"No." And Sister Ann smiled facetiously. "You might say that this is alien corn." The farmer did not smile back. "You don't happen to have any Pabst Blue Ribbon with you?"

"Got a bottle of Dr Pepper under the seat."

"I suppose that will do. Do you mind?"

Sister Ann spoke a parable while the farmer fetched the bottle from his truck. Most of the parable was lost in the wind that bent down the foot-high corn.

"You don't figure on building a church or nothing?" the farmer said.

"I'm waiting for a miracle," said Sister Ann pleasantly. "Would you mind leaving the bottle by my feet there? I'll drink it later."

The next Sunday, the Fundamentalist preacher denounced Sister Ann as a fraud. He was able to quote seventeen minutes of scriptures that proved beyond a reasonable doubt that anyone standing in a cornfield, particularly a woman, could be in no way considered a messenger of the Lord. No one could remember anyone claiming that Sister Ann was a messenger of the Lord, but then the Fundamentalist preacher was known to like to keep one step ahead of everyone. He even suggested that Sister Ann might well be Communist-inspired.

Sister Ann was situated two miles north of the village, which had eleven unpainted buildings and a Shell service station on its dirty main street.

A cult, small but powerful, led by the wife of the sheriff, began to worship Sister Ann. In the late spring dusk they would sit in the ditch across the fence from her and sing hymns while Sister Ann glowed golden in the sunset.

Some afternoons the landowner would bring a six-pack of Pabst Blue Ribbon to Sister Ann. He quizzed her about the kind of miracle she expected. She indicated that she might tell him if he brought a case of twelve.

The Fundamentalist preacher declared that the gates of heaven were closed to anyone who associated with Sister Ann.

Sister Ann's congregation held a bake sale at the community hall and with the proceeds bought fifteen concrete blocks which they piled near Sister Ann. Her congregation gave up wearing shoes.

Late one night a tall stranger in a flowing white robe approached Sister Ann. Sister Ann raised her weathered white gown above her waist. Her curls were the same burnished yellow as her hair. The moon turned her ecstatic eyes golden.

The sheriff's wife and her friends, with great difficulty, sacrificed a lamb to Sister Ann. It was July and hard to find a manageable lamb. Secondly, none of them, these solemn-faced housewives with flat chests and overbites, had ever sacrificed a lamb before. It got away twice before they finally did it in.

Sister Ann demurely raised her right hand, fist clenched.

"There is safety in numbers," she said.

The pile of concrete blocks grew. The landowner came nearly every day with a case of twelve. Sister Ann refused his advances.

The Fundamentalist preacher declared that Sister Ann was rooted to the ground with roots that ran clear down to the Devil. The Monday following that sermon his church burned down.

Sister Ann's belly swelled in the brilliant summer sun.

Teenagers raced their hotrods down the highway each night, letting up on the gas and allowing the cars to backfire as they passed Sister Ann. Pubescent boys began to walk out from the village. As darkness fell they would creep self-consciously from the opposite ditch, cautiously, like animals expecting to be spooked.

"You know what I got in my pants, lady?" the most adventurous said.

"Jesus loves you," replied Sister Ann.

"It's pink and rhymes with think . . . ," the boy said, and laughed. His breath like rotting apples.

"There were giants in the earth . . . ," said Sister Ann. "Genesis 6:4."

The boy exposed himself. Behind him his friends gasped.

"Pink, think, wink, mink . . . ," he chanted.

"Suffer the little children," said Sister Ann.

Like a rubber doll in an oven, the boy melted to a pink puddle and disappeared into the earth. The other boys stampeded away down the highway, their running shoes making the flapping sounds of startled wings.

In the cold October wind the cornstalks rustled like brown paper. From the village an entourage ambled up the highway: pickup trucks, a car or two, a tractor pulling a wagon full of hay. The laughter of children pierced the blue-black of the night. Sister Ann's congregation were safely locked in the jail. Torches were lit. An occasional tine glinted silver, the odd gun barrel glowed smoky blue. There was a gasoline drum in the box of the lead pickup.

From the field behind her, Sister Ann of the Cornfields heard the prehistoric rumble of the machine gobbling the dried cornstalks and at the same time goring the earth. The machine's eyes tunneled through the fall night.

A teenage boy, filled with bravado, crossed the ditch and leapt the fence. A smooth-handled three-pronged pitchfork glinted in his hands. As he raised it like a spear, the tines turned to milk, the icy metal ran down his arms and rolled like quicksilver along the denim of his jeans.

The landowner, smelling of snuff, his belly protruding against his overalls, leaned on the fence. "Why don't you just come along with us, Miss," he said. The boy stood frozen, the smooth white handle drawn back in his hand. Behind him the villagers babbled.

"You gonna be in a lot of trouble if you don't come along," the landowner said. He gestured toward the people behind him, their faces glowing red from the torches, and at the machine chuffing toward Sister Ann's back.

"Why don't we wait and see?" said Sister Ann, a fragment of moon touching her golden eyes.

The
Grecian
Urn

CHAPTER ONE

A Japanese red herring

The mail slot in the door to my house is taped open. It measures $9^1/_2''$ × $1^1/_4''$ and is $11''$ above the step. There is an empty Japanese orange box on the front step, and a three-inch-thick foam pillow on the floor just inside the door. I have placed food and water on the floor at strategic locations throughout the house, in red plastic dishes that once belonged to our cat.

My son argues that with winter fast approaching it is uneconomical to have the mail slot taped open. He is nineteen, in second year university, majoring in civil engineering and doing very well. He has a very attractive girlfriend named Tanya, with a dark red, pouty mouth and exceedingly large breasts.

My son often asks just exactly what it is that I expect to come through the slot. I tell him to trust his father.

Recently, and inexplicably to everyone but myself, I have committed some rather bizarre little crimes. To explain to the authorities the perfectly logical reasons for my criminal activity would, as I see it, be far worse than simply accepting the consequences. Explanation would cause me to reveal a story far too ludicrous to be believed. It is, I contend, far better to let everyone concerned assume that for reasons unknown, I Charles Bristow, age forty-nine, have gone a little, no, more than a little, strange. I am, I must admit, a particularly inept criminal. It is, I suppose, because I have had no practice. Until very recently I was a most average member of the community.

Suddenly becoming a criminal, and an inept one at that, is to say the least a traumatic experience. As a sort of last resort, perhaps in the way of therapy, although I am not at all sure about that, I am doing my best to convince everyone except my son that I am mentally deranged. I think I am going to try to blame my misfortune on the male menopause, about which I read a very interesting article in a back issue of the *Reader's Digest*.

A few weeks ago, if anyone had told me that I would be attempting to convince people that I am insane, I would have laughed at them. Widowed for some two years, I lived quietly in my own home, mortgage-free, with my son. I was employed as a minor bureaucrat in the city civil service, and had held my position for some thirty years. I am currently under suspension without pay, pending disposition of the criminal charges against me. I gardened, bowled Tuesday nights, attended a church-sponsored friendship gathering on Saturday evenings, and subscribed to a book of the month club.

As yet I have refused to discuss Allan or the urn while I am being held for psychiatric evaluation here at the J. Walter Ives Institute for the Emotionally Disturbed. Everyone knows about the urn. No one knows about Allan. The first time I was arrested, the night I broke the Grecian Urn, I was let out on bail, charged with willful damage and possession of burglar tools, to wit: a hammer and chisel. The next time the charge was trespassing by night, followed by loitering, followed by a second trespassing by night charge, at which time my bail was rescinded and I was remanded in custody for fourteen days for psychiatric evaluation. Seven of those days have passed.

I have submitted to a battery of tests: described my feelings toward my parents, tried to remember if I was bottle- or breast-fed, played with blocks and looked at ink blots.

Unthinkingly, I chose to use the hospital phone to call my son and plead with him to leave the mail slot open. When all rational arguments failed I ordered him to leave it open, reminding him that I paid his tuition to university as well as the utility bills.

My son complains that Tanya won't come to the house since she learned of my strange behavior. I sympathize with him. She used to come over Tuesdays and Saturdays, my nights out. It was seldom mentioned between us, but I could always tell because the air would be heavy with her perfume when I arrived home. Soon after Tanya began visiting our home regularly, my son took to washing his own sheets. I am quite proud of him.

The phone was apparently tapped. The doctors were smiling like slit throats the next day. They must also have talked to my son, for they were inordinately interested in the Japanese orange box on the front step. I denied everything, even phoning my son. However, during the interview I doodled a number of Japanese flags on the paper in front of me and also wrote Remember Pearl Harbor in a tiny, cramped hand, quite unlike my own. As I left the room, nonchalantly whistling "Over There," they converged on the paper like baying hounds.

At supper that evening, when a Toyota commercial came on the television, I began flipping carrots at the TV.

CHAPTER TWO

The All-Blue streetcar

I suppose it was logical that Allan should have come to me for help. Outside of Viveca I was probably the only living person who knew. Beatrice may have suspected but we never discussed the matter.

Allan's secret. What exactly is it that I know? That seems to be a real point of contention. I really only know what Allan has told me and what I think I have seen.

I never liked Allan. I didn't like him in 1943 and I don't like him today. I do like Viveca. I would do anything for Viveca. She was the only reason I tried to help Allan.

I have lived in this city all my life. I joined the army on my sixteenth birthday, October 3, 1942. Two months later I met Allan, or rather Allan sought me out as a friend. He was lonely. I have never liked to be unkind to anyone. I tolerated him. He had the look of an English schoolboy, cheeks like two apples floating in a pail of white paint, very blond hair, pale blue eyes, a mouth that looked like he was wearing lipstick.

"My parents came over when the war started. Money, you know. Horrified that I joined up."

I was noncommittal.

"I can do some rather unusual things," he said.

I started to tell him I was not interested but instead remained silent.

"My family is unique," he persisted. "We all have powers. They begin at puberty, reach full potential by about thirty, then decline to nothing by fifty."

"So what?" I said. My father fought with the IRA, claimed to have killed seven Black and Tans. "There'll Always Be an England" was not my favorite song. Allan was somehow insulted that he could not rouse my curiosity, but it didn't keep him at bay for long. He offered no demonstration of his uniqueness. I continued to reluctantly accept him as my friend. It was a few weeks later, on top of a railway trestle, in a streetcar that had jumped the tracks, that I got to observe Allan in action.

The All-Blue streetcar was not, as the name may suggest, painted blue. Instead of having names and destinations the streetcars bore small metal plates about a foot square on the front and rear. If one wished to get around the city, one learned quickly that the All-Blue streetcar traveled west to south, the Red-and-White streetcar went east to south, while the Green-and-Red went east to west.

On a dismal March night in 1943 we were traveling to a movie on the south side of the city. The All-Blue streetcar had to cross the river valley on top of a railway bridge. Halfway across the car bucked and pitched sideways. We were seated, Allan and I, at about the middle of the car, the only other passengers two girls about our age who were sitting at the very back. I thought we were certainly going to die. I could already feel the streetcar hurtling the four hundred feet toward the ice of the river below. The lights went out as the car swung sideways, the rear of the car hanging out over the water. At the last instant the front wheels caught on the outside track and the car hung, balancing like a poorly constructed teeter-totter. The conductor scrambled to safety. Allan and I edged toward the front. I looked back. The two girls were huddled together in the back corner. An instant later they were beside us and the four of us climbed from the front of the car, the white-faced motorman helping us down onto the deck of the bridge.

There is documentation of the incident, if not of Allan's act of moving the girls to safety. On the front page of the March 15, 1943 issue of a long-extinct daily newspaper is a photograph of two servicemen and two girls. My copy, yellow with age, is framed and hangs on the wall of my bedroom. The photograph was captioned The Survivors. The short blond youth with the chipmunk cheeks is Allan, the taller, rawboned young man is me. The girls! If I could produce even one of them to document the events of that night. One person in the world who could testify that my recent actions are not those of a madman. The girl beside me in the photo, the pale, blondish girl about whose waist I have my arm, protecting her as best I could from the bitter wind, is Beatrice. We were married in 1946. She died in 1974. The girl beside Allan, the one with green eyes and wine-colored hair spreading over her shoulders, is Viveca.

CHAPTER THREE

J. Walter Ives is a transvestite

Day nine. I have taken to writing short notes and dropping them around the hospital. The attendants are all spies as are most of the inmates.

Last night, they brought into my room a whimpering drunk who smelled like wet newspaper.

"Why are you here?" he asked me. He had little red eyes like a rat. A spy's question if I ever heard one.

"I go around killing drunks," I said, which ended the conversation.

My first note read: I am capable of great destruction. It was signed with a triangular Japanese flag. Triangles have great significance to the doctors here. At every opportunity I work the conversation around to the male menopause. A black doctor with an Afro moustache and a red-and-yellow caftan listened for some time before saying, "I'm a rat man myself, and rats don't have no male menopause. I don't believe in none of that jive."

Beware the Ides of March, I left taped to my pillow. That afternoon one of the doctors carried a copy of *Julius Caesar* with many little bookmarks in it.

Isn't everybody a chipmunk? I wrote that on a piece of cardboard and slipped it into a deck of playing cards in the

recreation room, in place of the jack of diamonds which I clev-
erly concealed in the toe of my slipper.

A large, jolly-looking man with bushy eyebrows and eyes
as blue as bachelor buttons sits beside me in the recreation
room. "I am a latent homosexual," he says, placing his hand on
my knee.

CHAPTER FOUR

Cosmo perfume

Neither Allan nor I ever saw any action during the war. We
spent our entire time stationed in our own city, although
those who joined up both before and after us were shipped off
to Europe, many never to return. Perhaps Allan had something to do with it. I never asked him. I am not a very curious
person.

After the adventure on the All-Blue streetcar, the four of us
became friends. I must reluctantly admit that of the two girls
I preferred Viveca. That, of course, was all it was, a preference.
Allan and Viveca became inseparable. Like Allan, Viveca was
an outgoing person. Besides being beautiful she had enormous
vitality. Beatrice was the quiet one. On the assumption that
likes attract we were paired together.

A significant, I believe that is the word Allan used to describe Viveca: no powers of her own, but extremely suscepti-
ble to his. Once or twice, when we were alone in barracks,
Allan gave small demonstrations of his abilities. He made objects fall from shelves, stopped and started my pocket watch
several times while seated in a chair across the room. Once he
shattered the glass in my shaving mirror simply by staring at
it. I was not particularly impressed. I asked if he could make
money. He said he couldn't. He said he could, if he wished,
dematerialize and inhabit inanimate objects. He said he could

live inside a silver dollar, or a tree, or the fender of a bus. He said that because of Viveca's susceptibility to his powers, he could allow her to experience the same phenomena. It seemed to me to be an extremely silly thing to do and I told him so.

Allan tried his best to convert me to his point of view. He said that he and Viveca would travel the world, being able to inhabit great works of art. He had, he said, the command of a dimension of which ordinary mortals were unaware. He not only could step into paintings or sculpture, but could come alive in the time and place that the work represented. It seemed like a lot of trouble to me. I envied Allan only Viveca. Once, at a dance hall, I took Viveca's hand to lead her to the dance floor. I could feel her pulse throbbing like something alive. She placed herself extraordinarily close to me as we danced. I could feel her breasts against the front of my uniform. Her perfume had the odor of cosmos, those tall pale pink and mauve flowers that sway beautifully in gardens like delicate children. I thought of kissing her. I'm certain she wouldn't have minded. But Allan would have, and Beatrice. I don't mean to belittle Beatrice. She was a good and faithful wife to me and as loving as her fragile health would permit. She gave me a fine son and many years of devotion.

"I wish things were different," I said to Viveca as we danced. "I wish that you and I might . . ."

She moved back slightly to look into my face. Her laugh was joyful, like wind chimes, and I remember her words, but I remember more the liquid green of her eyes and the pink tip of her tongue peeking between her lips.

"Dear Charles," she said. "You are of another world."

After the war ended we saw less and less of Allan and Viveca. Sometime late in 1945 they left and we never heard from them again. That is until the night before I was first arrested.

CHAPTER FIVE

Only you Dick daring . . .

It was Viveca who came to the door. She was eighteen when I had last seen her, she looked no more than twenty-five now; twenty-six, she told me later. It was, she had decided, the ideal age. She held her hand out to me. The pulse was there, throbbing like a bird between us.

It embarrassed me to see her looking so young. I have not aged particularly gracefully. It would be a kindness to say that I have the average appearance of a man dramatically close to fifty.

Viveca spent little time on amenities. Allan was in trouble, she told me, and because Allan was in trouble so was she. They needed the help of a third party. Would I be it?

I am sure that Allan, with his inordinate perceptions, knew how I felt about Viveca. That was why he sent her ahead. He knew I could refuse her nothing. It was quite extraordinary, her reappearance after some thirty years. In recent times, and especially since my wife passed away, I have been fantasizing more and more about Viveca. I remember Allan once describing to me certain, to say the least, avant-garde, sexual practices, and intimating rather strongly that he and Viveca . . .

"Allan must talk with you," Viveca said.

I agreed. Allan was like Dorian Grey; he looked scarcely older than when I last saw him. Side by side we could be mistaken for father and son. There was a desperate tone in his voice as he talked to me, a sense of urgency with just a hint of panic. I found great pleasure in Allan's distress. I tried to remain very calm and feign disinterest, but secretly I was greatly stimulated. I recalled Viveca in my arms, Allan talking of his uniqueness disappearing at age fifty. Perhaps, just perhaps, there was a chance. I would pretend to help but then at the last moment . . . As my father was known to say, a stiff cock

73

knows no conscience. I would have followed Viveca over Niagara Falls in a teacup.

His powers were virtually gone, Allan explained. He and Viveca had spent the last thirty years doing exactly as they said they would. They had passed like needles through the history of the world. They had visited nearly every time and civilization by means of inhabiting paintings and other original works of art. With Allan's time running out they had decided on a final resting place: a Grecian Urn that was the feature exhibit of a traveling display currently showing at our museum. It was, Allan stated, the urn to which John Keats had written his immortal "Ode on a Grecian Urn." I had no reason to doubt him as I had seen it advertised as such in our newspaper.

"Why me?" I asked. "Surely you've made this transfer of dimension thousands of times before?"

It seemed that they had attempted the transfer a few weeks before, in another city, and failed. Allan had been able to send Viveca on her journey but had no energy left to transport himself, and had barely been able to return Viveca to her natural form. They wanted me along as a safeguard in case something went wrong again. A mere precaution, they assured me. Allan had been conserving his energy for several weeks and everything would go well. Both went into ecstasies about the life ahead of them on the urn. The tranquillity, beauty, peace, they sounded to me like acquaintances of mine who had recently taken up organic gardening. They quoted lavishly from Keats's poem, assured me that they both realized that they would be totally unable to cope with the everyday world without Allan's powers, and that the ultimate in nth dimensional living was waiting for them on the urn.

I was not about to argue with them although my mind was in turmoil. I tried to think of ways that I could trick Allan into leaving Viveca behind. However, I am hardly a devious person, and as I watched Viveca's face as she described the joys that lay ahead of her, her eyes flashed, and she laughed often, the magic bell-like laughter of long ago. Her perfume was the same and my thoughts moved to the rows and rows of gentle cosmos that had graced my garden the last few summers. I would help them both. It would be the last act of love I could ever perform for Viveca.

CHAPTER SIX

The importance of triangles

Day twelve. Had a long session with one of the doctors today. He reviewed the results of my tests.

"You are as sane as I am," he told me.

He is the one with the copy of *Julius Caesar*, who puts great stock in the importance of triangles.

CHAPTER SEVEN

Blue gnats

The three of us visited the museum that same evening. The Grecian Urn was the central exhibit. They pointed out to me the spot they intended to occupy on the urn. They were as happy as if they were merely going on a holiday. I have a scant knowledge of art, but even to my untrained eye the urn was impressive. It stood some four feet high and there were three bands on it, each displaying a number of raised figures in Greek dress, in various postures, among pastoral scenery.

I arranged to accompany them to the museum the following night. It was difficult to get close to the urn. It was behind crimson ropes and there was a constant line of people filing past. We waited until closing time. The circular hall was empty. Allan shook hands with me and gave me a few last moment instructions. Viveca kissed me, her mouth a swarming thing. Was I wrong to interpret the kiss as much more than one old friend saying goodbye to another?

"Would you check the exit-way, Charles," Allan said to me.

I walked the length of the red carpet to the doorway, looked outside to be certain that we were alone. When I turned Allan and Viveca were gone: all that was left for me to see was a small swarm of bluish stars no larger than gnats disappearing into the side of the urn in a tornado shape. The urn was several feet distant from the restraining ropes. I looked carefully around, crawled under the ropes and approached the urn. In the area that Allan and Viveca had pointed out to me were two new figures, a boy and a girl, looking as though they had been part of the urn since it was created. The operation appeared to have been a success. I was just bending to inspect them closely when a startled security guard entered the display hall.

"What are you doing?" he demanded.

I stuttered an illogical reply.

"The museum is closed for the night, sir," he said with an air of authority. He looked carefully at me, then all around the exhibit hall. "I thought I heard voices," he said. "Are you sure you're alone?"

"I was checking for gnats," I said, and laughing hysterically, fled from the building.

CHAPTER EIGHT

The limits of psychiatry

Day thirteen. Another session with the doctors. Three listened; one spoke. The spokesman's eyes were small hazel triangles. Their consensus of opinion was that I am trying to con them.

After a long discussion about doctor-patient relationships, I admitted that I was trying to con them, and told them the complete story from start to finish. Then I asked their advice. They suggested that when I go to court I plead temporary insanity and not try to tell the judge my story.

"He might think you're crazy," the spokesman said.
They intend to certify me sane. Something is wrong.

CHAPTER NINE

Meanwhile, back at the museum

Twice the following evening I went through the lineup to view the urn. It was impossible for me to get beyond the re-straining ropes. I merely stood and stared at the figures on the third band of the urn until the people behind pushed me on. Allan had given me certain instructions to follow and in order to do my job I had to get very close to Allan and Viveca. I had no choice but to wait until the museum closed. I hid in an al-cove, then at the first opportunity rushed to the urn. I looked closely at the new figures. They seemed to fit in well. I traced the outline of Viveca's body with my index finger. As in-structed I put my ear close to the figures.

"Help!" hissed Allan in the voice of a movie cartoon mouse.

"What's wrong?"

"Everything. This urn is not genuine. Seventeenth century at the latest. No character. No dimension . . ."

"There's no one around. Come on out."

"I can't."

"Why not?"

"My powers are weak. It may be weeks, even months . . ."

"You'll just have to rest up."

"The urn is being moved to another city day after tomor-row . . . and by the way keep your hands off Viveca, I saw what you did."

"Viveca's being awfully quiet."

As I spoke I touched Viveca again. I could feel her warmth and smell the faint odor of cosmos.

"Remember it is I who maintain her in this dimension," he said in an agitated voice, like a tape being played at the wrong speed. Then he told me what I must do. Detailed instructions on how to rescue him and Viveca. He had barely finished when the security guard appeared.

"You again," he said.

"It is such a treasure," I said. "I only wanted to get a close look at it."

"If I catch you around here again I'm going to have to take you in."

I apologized for inconveniencing him and slunk away.

The following evening I hid in the washroom of the museum. Feeling like a fool, I stood on a toilet seat when the security guard checked the washroom at closing time. After waiting a suitable length of time I took the hammer and chisel that Allan had instructed me to bring and made my way to the urn.

Ever so carefully I worked at chipping the two small figurines from the face of the urn. I deliberately released Viveca first, placed her gently in the side pocket of my suit, then went to work to free Allan. As I had his figure nearly liberated, my chisel slipped ever so slightly and the urn cracked and split into a number of pieces. I managed to catch Allan as the urn disintegrated. Remarkably, his only injury was a very small piece broken from his right foot.

Regardless of what the security guard told the police, it was not me who was screaming and cursing incoherently. At the sound of the urn breaking and Allan screaming in his tiny voice, the security guard ran into the exhibit area. He said something original like "What's going on here?" Then he drew his pistol and pointed it very unsteadily at me. I bent over and placed Allan among the ruins of the urn. "You had better put up your hands," said the guard as he advanced on me. I complied.

"Come over here with me so I can watch you while I call the police," he said, pointing to a desk and chairs a few yards distant. He looked at me closely. "You're the man who was talking to the urn." He was about sixty, pink-cheeked, with a military haircut and a small white moustache like a skiff of snow below his nose. On his dark blue uniform he wore a name tag: Charles Stoddard—Security.

"Dear Charles," I said. "You are of another world."

CHAPTER TEN

After the fall

The day after I was first arrested I stayed home from work. It was the first day I had missed in eight years. I told my son I had gotten drunk and fallen against the urn and that I had no idea why I was in the museum. He looked at me skeptically for he knows that I virtually never drink. My lawyer, the one I called to post bail for me the previous night, insisted at the time I submit to a breath analysis. My blood-alcohol reading was 0.00%.

CHAPTER ELEVEN

Putting a cloud in a suitcase

They are holding Viveca as evidence. I was searched at the police station after my arrest. I'm afraid I made rather a fool of myself.

"It's a religious object," I wailed. "You can't deny me my religion."

"Looks like a piece of the vase he busted," said a young cop. He was built like a middle guard and looked like a teenager. The whole police force was very young.

"Be brave, Viveca," I said to her as I passed her to the police officer. I could feel her pulse beating very rapidly. The middle guard slipped her into an envelope and licked the flap with a beefy tongue.

I demanded that he leave air holes in the envelope. I'm afraid I may have become a little hysterical about it. Reluctantly he took a pen and poked a few holes in the envelope.

"You're not going to put her in a safe! You mustn't put her in an airtight place of any kind." I tried to remain composed, but my voice was quite out of control.

"Trust me, Mr. Bristow," the officer said.

"You can call a lawyer now," the man on the desk informed me. Then turning to one of the officers, said, "It must be a full moon. They come out from under their rocks whenever there's a full moon."

The moment I got home I taped open the mail slot and made the other preparations I have described. While the security guard was phoning the police, Allan limped from the display area to the far wall, and while the deceased urn was being examined and I was being handcuffed and led out of the museum he slipped along the baseboard and out the front doors. I can only assume that he will try to make his way back to my home. It doesn't seem reasonable that he will go anywhere else, for it will be very difficult for a four-inch-tall plaster figure about three-eighths of an inch thick to get much attention from anyone who does not believe in him. Allan gave me so many instructions that after my arrest they all seemed to have blurred and merged with the actual conversations I had with Allan and Viveca. I do seem to recall him saying that after his removal from the urn he would require nourishment, but I can't be certain. I put out food and water just in case.

Now that I'm willing to tell the truth I find it would be easier to stuff a cloud into a suitcase than to get anyone to take me seriously. I pleaded with my lawyer to have Viveca returned to me. I told him to have the museum people check and they would find that she was not a part of the broken urn. He promised he would look into it but from the tone of his voice I could tell he was humoring me. From the hospital I phoned the museum director and pleaded with him to view the piece of evidence the police were holding. I insisted that he compare it with photographs of the urn. I'm afraid I may have become a little hysterical again. He took no action, I suppose considering the source of the call. Over the telephone I have become quite friendly with the middle guard at the police station, his name is Rourke and our families come from a similar part of Ireland. He assures me that Viveca is being kept in an airy bottom drawer.

CHAPTER TWELVE

Meanwhile, back at J.W.I.

I keep having a dream. Sometimes I have it in the daytime, therefore I suppose I would have to say it is a fantasy as well as a dream. The water dishes that I left in my house for Allan's use are large red plastic ones. They are some four inches off the ground. Since Allan is only about four inches tall, my calculations indicate that he would have great difficulty getting a drink without falling in. I should phone my son and have him change the dishes for saucers. Yet I do not. My dream is that my son phones me to say that he has found (a) a four-inch plaster figure in Greek dress submerged in the water dish, or (b) a full-grown man of about fifty who must have had an extremely difficult time drowning himself in less than three inches of water.

Assuming that doctors like to hear about dreams I discussed this one with them. They are not concerned because they don't believe my original story. Their professional advice is to try not to think about it.

The night following my first arrest I went back to the museum grounds to look for Allan. My concern was not really for Allan but that he is the only one who can release Viveca. I spent a good deal of time searching the foliage around the building and skulking about the grounds, until a greasy-looking kid with a widow's peak, driving a Toyota with a frothing Doberman in the back seat, shone a spotlight on me. Trespassing by night. The following afternoon I was arrested for loitering about the grounds. I tried to be more careful that night but the kid with the Doberman got me again, hence my banishment to J. Walter Ives.

CHAPTER THIRTEEN

Sayonara

My fourteen days are up. The doctors come to say goodbye. They explain that according to their analysis of my handwriting I am perfectly sane.

"There are other dimensions," I assure them, "of which you are incapable of understanding. In fact . . ."

I am interrupted by the head nurse who advises me that there is a phone call from my son. The head nurse says that he sounds very agitated.

Mankiewitz
Won't Be Bowling
Tuesday Nights Anymore

*W*hen he found out that
Manny was going to die,
Bert didn't feel the way he knew he should, the way he knew
everyone else would feel. Friends for twenty years, yet the
sense of impending loss was tempered . . . by what? Bert was
sorry for Manny, but thankful that it was Manny and not him.
Where was the grief?

What Bert did feel was a sense of exhilaration, and he
couldn't understand it. He tried to feel differently but could
barely control his excitement; he was actually looking forward to telling everyone the news. He was already planning
Manny's funeral.

> *The Management and Staff*
> *of Comanche Cabs Inc.*
> *wish you a speedy recovery.*

The least they could have done was have one of the drivers
deliver the flowers. To start with you didn't send a guy like

Manny flowers. You sent him a bottle or a box of cigars even if you knew he couldn't have them. The card was written by the florist. It was just so impersonal.

"Hell, I'da delivered the things myself if somebody'd told me about them," Bert said out loud as he worked the cab through traffic toward home, "but nobody ever tells me anything anymore." He could see Manny's arms, pale and white as the hospital shirt, the veins sticking out, looking blue and cold. Manny was skin and bone: his voice that was always so strong, now barely a whisper. The doctors gave him maybe six weeks.

When Manny, after months of "stomach trouble," finally got around to going to the doctors, they told him he had ulcers and had to have an operation.

"He's been looking like death warmed over for nearly six months," Bert told anybody who would listen. "I bet it's something a lot worse." And it was.

"They did an exploratory," Manny's wife told Bert over the phone, "just closed him up again, there's nothing they can do. He knows, so you don't have to act phony around him."

But Bert did act phony. Even after all the years there was nothing for them to talk about and neither mentioned the fact that Manny was never coming out of the hospital. Bert would stand with his hands in his jacket pockets, embarrassed by the silence. He felt that his visits made Manny tense, so he kept them short.

"We should have had a clue when he stopped joking over the air," Bert said to Crabby. "It's been months since he called me the old man, or asked you if you knew the way to the airport, or asked Schmidt how come he'd missed him in the war." In the old days, when they used to joke a lot on the air, Bert called Manny "the Kid." They were the oldest of the driver-owners. At sixty, Manny had two years on him.

When they started the company six years before, there were only the four of them: Bert and Mankiewitz, Crabby and Schmidt. Crabby's wife dispatched from his house. They each worked twelve-hour shifts, and if somebody wanted a day off they were on call for twenty-four. Because they stayed with it, the business grew. Cab companies came and went, but they were all determined that they were never going to work for Orangeaid, or anybody else, ever again.

Eventually they opened an office and hired a dispatcher, a stolid English lady who lisped and reversed numbers. They brought in a couple of new owners. Drivers and dispatchers came and went regularly until they hired a girl named Colleen. As far as Bert was concerned she had as much to do with the success of the business as anyone. It was her voice. She was a slight little girl with loose red curls and a million freckles; she came to work in blue jeans trailing a great black dog named Jasper which sometimes barked into the microphone, but she had the voice of a meadowlark. She wasn't a great dispatcher, but she giggled at her mistakes, and even surly old Schmidt had to admit he liked her. She was good for business. Bert knew because of the number of compliments he got from passengers who always said how sweet and helpful she was on the phone. "Hey, I'd sure like to meet that chick," said all the drunks he carted home, and they'd call the company just to talk to her, or ride in the cab just to listen to her voice on the two-way.

After Conklin became manager the dispatching was contracted out to a professional answering service, where a bevy of severe middle-aged ladies who looked and sounded alike cawed like crows and discouraged unnecessary chatter on the air. "They are very efficient," said Conklin. Bert missed the meadowlark girl's laughter.

Conklin started as the firm's accountant. He was a bugger for detail. Bert never liked him. He was always coming up with ideas to make more money, but the ideas always seemed to take some of the joy out of the business. Like the cars. At first as long as it was a four-door it could get on the fleet: Bert had a black Rambler, Crabby a white Chev, Manny and Schmidt both had Plymouths. They put plastic signs on the doors that read Comanche Cabs, and a top-light whatever shape the shop had in stock. Now that there were twenty-four in the fleet, all were Plymouth Furys, all white, all with the same shaped top-light, all with the scarlet Comanche Cabs logo printed down both sides, with the stylized headdress on the C. Everyone rented their radios from the same firm, dealt at the same service station, carried the same sign on the trunk advertising a local radio station, for which the company got free commercials. Conklin was an organizer, but it wasn't like working for yourself anymore.

Bert envisioned the reactions he would get when he told people that Manny was cashing in. Everybody, he was certain, would be shocked and would want to do whatever they could for Manny. As the days passed Bert couldn't believe what he saw and heard. It wasn't that Manny wasn't well liked. In all the years he'd known him Bert had never heard anyone say anything unkind about Manny. Herbert L. Mankiewitz was always hale and hearty with a kind word for everyone. Even Schmidt, who was always quarreling with the dispatchers and was getting paranoid lately, accusing the dispatchers of saving only short fares for him, and the other owners of plotting against him, exempted Manny.

"Manny, he don't want to hurt nobody," said Schmidt.

When Bert told Conklin, the first thing he said was, "Who's going to buy his car?" He expected that from Conklin, but not from Crabby.

"That's too bad," Crabby said, without nearly as much feeling as Bert thought he should show. "It catches up with all of us sometime. I wonder who he's gonna sell his cab to?"

Bert was tempted to scream at him. "He's your friend. We started this lousy company. He could pick up a fare at four A.M. on an empty street with ten cars cruising ahead of him. He went to the airport three times for your one. He stole so many fares from the Orangeaid stand that Drupopilis said he was going to have Manny's car painted orange on one side. Who gives a damn who's gonna buy his car."

But what he said was, "Conklin's one up on you. He's already got an option, through his lawyer of course. He didn't even go up to see Manny himself. Gave him a good price though, I gotta say that for him."

Bert figured he'd have to help Manny's old lady screen the visitors, figured they'd be coming in droves. Crabby and Schmidt went once, together. Otherwise there was just Bert and Manny's family.

They'd bowled together on a team sponsored by O'Brien Engineering. O'Brien and his two partners filled out the team. In the old days Comanche Cabs had their own team but Bert and Manny were all that was left. The new owners worked their shift and went home to their families. They weren't cabbies, they were goddamned executives who cried like babies if they had to work a twelve-hour shift.

And not one of the bastards wore hats, Bert thought. What was a cabbie without a hat? Manny and Bert wore the black peaked caps with TAXI in silver letters across the band. Schmidt wore his little felt cap to keep his bald skull warm, but even Crabby was going bareheaded these days. And the drivers, long-haired college kids who couldn't care less. Not like the old days when there were some real characters. Like Fatty Sullivan, the guy drove for years before the licensing board discovered that he had a wooden leg. Drove a gear-shift car, and a goddamned good driver too.

Manny was a pretty fair bowler but he tended to panic, especially during the Schlitz frame, usually the fifth, when they bowled to see who bought beer. Even if he was working on a turkey, Manny would come up with a four- or five-pin count on the first ball of the Schlitz frame. He bought about three out of five times.

God, Bert thought, was that to be Manny's epitaph . . . he was a pretty fair bowler, but he panicked in the Schlitz frame?

Bert had a brainstorm. The bowling-league trophy didn't have a real name. It was just called the Industrial League

Trophy. And it was a grand one, about three feet tall with seven golden bowlers in a pyramid shape. They'd name it the Herbert L. (Manny) Mankiewitz Memorial Trophy. Manny's name would live on all right. He'd suggest it to O'Brien, who was also president of the league, when they started bowling again in September. Yeah, that was a real good idea.

"Car 20, Orangeaid to 6."

"10-4, 20."

"Car 18, 10-2 OK?"

"10-4, 18. Keep it down to an hour."

As Bert drove toward the hospital he listened to the chatter of the two-way radio. The 10-code was the one part of the taxi business that always intrigued his passengers.

"How do you know what's being said?" they asked.

Bert would eye the passenger and estimate the amount of tip he'd get if he gave a complete explanation. Then he'd grin and translate good-naturedly.

"Car 20, Orangeaid to 6, means that Car 20 has ripped off a fare from the stand of our chief competitor, Empire Taxi. In the trade they're known as Orangeaid because of the color of their cars. 10-4 means yes or acknowledged. The 6 means the zone. We have the city divided into a grid with nine zones so the drivers can tell the dispatcher the general area they are going to."

"What was she telling him to keep down to an hour?"

"Lunch. 10-2 means lunch. 10-3 coffee. 10-5 washroom. 10-7 out for a minute. 10-8 back in. 10-20 asks for directions. 10-200 asks for the police. 10-33 is an emergency. 55 is a polite way of saying shut up. 99 is permission to end your shift."

They'd drink it all in and not be much wiser than when he started, but they'd pretend to understand and give him a good tip which was what paid the rent.

Bert pictured the funeral. And a grand event it would be. He could see the twenty-four white cabs all freshly washed and shined, moving in a dignified procession behind the contrasting black funeral cars. People would stop what they were doing and look.

"They must have really respected that guy," they'd say. "He must have been a good cab driver."

Bert got choked up just thinking about it. There would be black crêpe on all the aerials. He'd talk to Conklin about it. Hell, the guys would go for that, somebody had probably suggested it already. They could sell it to Conklin because it would be good advertising, Bert reasoned. But when Bert suggested it Conklin practically bust a gut.

"Do you realize how much it would cost us to do that? We'd have to pass almost a thousand calls to the opposition if we took all our cars off the road for an afternoon, and you can bet there would be a certain percentage of that business we'd never get back. Besides, Mankiewitz isn't dead yet."

"He will be."

"I don't know. I had an uncle they gave up on a couple of times. He's still living."

"Have you seen him lately?" Bert knew the answer but he hoped he might embarrass Conklin a little. That afternoon Manny's eyes had been kind of dull and lifeless, and his two-day beard was like a skiff of snow on his face.

"No. Haven't had time."

"Well I have. He hasn't got more than a week left."

"You let me know a couple of days before the funeral. I'll line up spare drivers for you and Crabby and any of the others that want to go to the funeral . . ."

Bert slammed out of the office.

He broached the subject with Crabby and some of the other drivers. "What's Conklin say?" was all they could ask.

"He says no."

"Well guess we'd better go along with him. We pay him to manage the company."

Bert called them out.

"I think Bert's taking it worse than Manny," he heard one of them say as he stalked away.

It had been more fun in the old days. Bert remembered their first direct line. Crabby had practically been living with the manager of the Centurian Bar for weeks. Finally, more to get rid of Crabby than anything else, he allowed them to install a direct line and promised them a few calls on a trial basis. They stationed one of the cars in the alley behind the Centurian and by the time they hung up the direct line a driver was in the bar looking for the fare. Orangeaid was giving half-hour service. Before long they had all the Centurian's business. Now, they had a direct line in almost every important bar and cocktail lounge in the city.

It wasn't like he owned a part of the company anymore. It was more like it had been when he drove for Orangeaid where Drupopilis owned all thirty cars. It was just like being an employee again. They worked hard when they first started but nobody told them what to do.

He remembered the first few months when they got most of their business by scooping fares from their competitor's stands. Then, while they had a captive audience, they'd give a pitch on why the fare should ride with Comanche in the future and press a business card into the fare's hand along with his change.

It was different then. Manny used to chase ambulances and the air was always humming with happy chatter. Manny was never happier than when he could get to an accident before the police. He would park his cab in the middle of an intersection, flashers blazing, and direct traffic until the authorities arrived. If he was really lucky he'd get to administer first aid to someone. Then he'd tell everyone about it over the two-way.

When the professional dispatchers took over they kept screeching "55" at poor old Manny. It just rolled off his back until in exasperation Conklin told Manny they were going to tape his mouth and make him tap his messages in Morse code. Manny was sort of afraid of "suits" like Conklin, and he was a lot quieter after that.

Bert asked Manny if he'd like to have a two-way in his room so he could listen to the taxi calls. Manny thought it would be a good idea. Manny was getting thinner every day. He had snow-white curly hair, blue eyes and a ruddy complexion. Bert's hair was white too, but it was straight and thinning on top. Even when Manny was healthy Bert outweighed him by about forty pounds, most of it carried just below his belt like a sack of flour.

Bert stood at the door of Conklin's office waiting for him to get off the phone. He was being so goddamned nice it was sickening to some customer who was complaining about something.

"Public relations is the key to success," Conklin told them at the owners' meetings. Conklin's office had thick carpet, a big desk with a glass top, and a real oil painting on the wall. The first office Comanche had was a basement room below a welding shop. The transmitter, one wooden chair, a broken-up desk with no bottom drawer, and a very old chair stuffed with horsehair where the guys who were off duty grabbed a minute or two's shut-eye. A map of the city was all that adorned the wall.

"Morning Conk," Bert said, knowing that he hated to be called Conk. The new owners and drivers called him Mr. Conklin, and he liked the oldtimers to call him T.J.

"Listen Conk, I want to take one of the radios out of the storeroom."

"What for?"

"I'm gonna take it up to Manny. He can tune in on the calls. He'll get a kick out of it."

"It's against Federal regulations to use a unit like that."

"Who's gonna know, for chrissakes?" Bert surmised that Conklin was inventing Federal regulations.

"I'd know. We don't want any trouble with the government."

"Come on Conklin, it's for Manny. I own part of this company too, you know."

"You own one twenty-fourth, Bert. Bring it up at the owners' meeting next month. If everybody else goes along it's okay with me."

"There ain't gonna be no next month for Manny."

"You can get him a CB receiver if you want to but you can't use company crystals." Bert slammed the door to Mr. Conklin's office as he left.

Bert rented a radio from the communications supplier, paid for company crystals out of his own pocket, took it up to the hospital and hooked it up for Manny.

"Got it out of the supply room," he told Manny. "Conk and the boys send their best."

The next morning when he was sure most of the owners were on the air Bert picked up his mike. "Hey guys, you can say Hi to Manny. He's got his own radio up at the hospital. If he's good I'm gonna get him his own mike so he can talk back to you."

"55," cawed the dispatcher.

The funeral was another disappointment. There were only about fifteen people there, mostly relatives. Bert's was the only company car, although Drupopilis was there with his orange Cadillac. For once Bert was happy to see him.

"I'm booking off now to go to the funeral," he said.

"Do you have a spare driver taking over, car 12?"

"Negative. I'm taking my car."

"You're supposed to finish your shift."

"Well I'm 99. So take me off the board."

"I don't know," said the dispatcher uncertainly.

Bert reached down and shut off the radio.

He was looking at but not seeing the six o'clock news when O'Brien phoned.

"The season's starting in a couple of weeks. You and Manny going to be bowling again?"

"I'll be bowling as usual," Bert said. As he spoke his vision of the Herbert L. (Manny) Mankiewitz Memorial Trophy faded away into the weather report.

"And Manny?"

"He's quit," Bert said. "Mankiewitz won't be bowling Tuesday nights anymore."

"Okay," said O'Brien.

A Picture
of the
Virgin

*T*he place where we went was known as American House. Edmonton was the jumping-off place for American troops going and coming on the Alaska Highway. There were always sizable contingents of American soldiers in Edmonton all during the war and even for a couple of years afterward. The American barracks were located in and around the Municipal Airport, which was and still is situated in the heart of the city.

It was Allan who suggested that we "get our ashes hauled." A typically English expression, I'm afraid, with no discernible intelligent meaning that I'm aware of. The first time he used it, I asked him what it meant, and he looked at me the way people have been looking at me all my life, with that slow upward motion of the head and that imitation roll of the eyes that says, "My God, how stupid you are. Everyone in the world but you knows . . ." Then he explained that it was a

94

euphemism for going to a whorehouse, and facetiously asked me if I knew what *that* meant.

We went. My girl was about twenty-five, a hawk-featured blonde with black roots who obviously thought she resembled Betty Grable, because she struck a Grable pinup pose in every doorway she chanced to encounter. She gave me the once-over with slate gray eyes, cold as a bird's, and dismissed whatever she thought she saw. Once we were inside the room, she was brisk in a bored sort of way, like a supermarket cashier. She gave me instructions to get undressed which I followed. I lay on the bed and she used her mouth on me. It did not bring me a great deal of pleasure. She had small even teeth which caused me a good deal of worry and she was what I considered to be very rough. Although, assuming she knew her job, I offered no complaint as she took me to an instant short of orgasm, stopped, lay back on the bed, hiked up the bluish kimono she was wearing, and instructed me to lie on top of her. I did. She used her hand to guide me into her, bucked her thin body a couple of times and I was finished. I was still breathing noisily into the shoulder of her kimono, which smelled of something like lighter fluid, when she slipped out from under me, went to the sink in the corner, and began to run the water. Her pubic hair matched her dark roots.

"You better get dressed," she said to me as if I had just purchased a loaf of bread and a quart of milk, "they'll be somebody else waiting for the room."

Possibly guessing that I was somewhat of a virgin, Allan had more or less told me what to expect. Although he was only a month or two older than me, he took great pains to elaborate on his many and varied sexual exploits, beginning for him at age nine and encompassing any number of young girls, as well as at least one headmaster's wife at a private school he attended.

My date, as Mrs. Burrell, the madam of American House, had called her, washed her hands, patted a small white towel between her thighs, then turned toward me where I was struggling back into my clothes, and with a little hop took a sitting position on the edge of the chipped white sink in the corner. She made a face to demonstrate the effect the cold porcelain had on her buttocks, adjusted herself and proceeded to pee in the sink. To say the least, I was dumbfounded.

"Ain't you ever seen a girl take a pee before?" she said with a small derisive laugh. As a matter of fact, I hadn't.

It was not a particularly memorable experience. However, it wasn't so unpleasant that I wouldn't try it again in hopes that it would be better. It seems to me analogous to my first bridge lesson. My father used to say something about anticipation being nine-tenths of the actual event, and in situations like this the real fun lay in the planning to go, wondering what it would be like, and all the strange and wonderful speculations that led up to the actual event.

American House was just south of the airport, I think on 106th Street. It was within a twenty-minute walk of where we were stationed. Allan was always able to mysteriously procure passes for us whenever we wanted to leave the base. When I asked how he accomplished it, he smiled his "My God but you're dumb" smile and changed the subject.

There are many stories about American House. I have no idea which are true and which the products of overactive imaginations. The madam, a Mrs. Burrell, Mrs. B to everyone, looked exactly the way I envisioned a madam should. She was a Hollywood stereotype madam: mid-fifties, dyed red hair cut short, too much makeup unsuccessfully covering the too-many lines on her face, a cigarette perpetually dangling from the corner of her mouth, one violet eye squinted up to keep the rising smoke at bay.

Rumor had it that her husband had worked in the Canadian National Railway yards roundhouse in Calder, an area on the city's northwest outskirts. Put in time was a more apt description, for he carried a piece-work quilt to work with him each night and slept seven hours of his eight-hour shift in an abandoned steam boiler. The rumor goes on to state that one night someone hooked up the steam boiler, broiled Mr. B and made Mrs. B a widow.

"He was done up tender as an overcooked chicken," she reportedly told an officer visiting American House. "They had a devil of a time dressing him for the funeral, his bones kept pulling out of the sockets every time they moved him even slightly."

Railroad pensions being small, Mrs. B began looking for a job and took on a distributorship for Corsetina Corsets. To satisfy her employer, she needed to employ a number of direct sales people and she regularly ran ads in the Help Wanted Female section of the Edmonton *Bulletin:*

Easy money, short hours,
call Rosalinda Burrell,
24712.

She made a marginal living from the corset franchise until she found that many of the women who applied for jobs were new to the city and in need of a place to stay. Her home had a number of extra bedrooms.

Her husband had had a grandiose dream of owning a Spanish hacienda, although he had never been farther south of Edmonton than Great Falls, Montana. He designed the building that was to become known as American House, did much of the work himself, but when the interior ground floor was finished, lost interest and did little or nothing the last few years of his life toward finishing the upstairs, landscaping, or putting the final coat of stucco on the outside. The house, of a vaguely Spanish American appearance, sprawled across two lots, gray as a prison with only the scratch-coat of stucco on front and back. For some reason the ends of the building had only lath and tarpaper. The once shiny black tarpaper was weathered to a soft mouse-gray, and frayed edges flapped like bird wings whenever the wind blew, which in Edmonton is most of the time.

After establishing that renting rooms was almost as profitable as selling corsets, Rosalinda Burrell began having the upstairs rooms finished. Always an economical person, she spent as little as possible, getting the less expensive sand finish on the interior walls and having a light fixture fastened to each ceiling. She put down institutional brown linoleum on the floors of the rooms and hall, installed a three-quarter Hollywood bed, a chest of drawers, and with a burst of unprecedented foresight, a second-hand sink in each room. At the north end of the building a flight of rough plank stairs ran down the outside like a fire escape. It was therefore possible to enter the front door, do your business on the second floor, and exit without mingling with the incoming guests.

Not long ago, a year perhaps, I went for a long walk one evening, and wandered the streets south of the airport until I found American House. It stood vacant, looking every bit as dilapidated as it did thirty years ago. I would have liked to have gone to a neighbor and inquired as to how long the house had been vacant and whatever became of Rosalinda Burrell. I, of course, didn't.

On perhaps our sixth or seventh visit to American House, I met Teddy. Allan and I came in the side door and found Mrs. B sitting at her kitchen table with her hourglasses lined up in front of her. They weren't exactly hourglass shaped, but each held exactly fifteen minutes worth of rose-colored sand. They sat in two rows on the table. If a room or girl was occupied, the hourglass was pulled about six inches forward and flipped to start the sand running. When one expired and the customer hadn't visibly departed or the girl come down to announce her availability, Mrs. B would climb the stairs to the second floor, knock on the door in question and call out "Time" in her deep gravelly voice.

I wonder what happened to those hourglasses? Surely they would have great value as antiques. I can visualize Mrs. B in her old age hobbling into one of those furniture-polish-smelling antique stores, her arms loaded with hourglasses full of pink sand.

She greeted Allan heartily, after all he was a regular customer, but looked at me as if I was a sack of flour.

"You remember Charles," Allan said.

Her blank stare told me that she didn't, although we had been to her house an equal number of times.

Off the kitchen was a small parlor almost like a doctor's waiting room, where, if all the girls were occupied, customers could wait. I was only in the waiting room once. It was dark and austere with a black bench along each wall, two ashtrays on chrome stands, a black wood coffee table covered with dog-eared magazines, and a dappled mirror on the wall. I chanced to stand up at the sound of footsteps coming down the outside stairs, an officer tapped the window and gave Mrs. B a mock salute. She pushed a still running hourglass with perhaps five minutes in it to the rear of the table, pulled a new one forward, flipped it to start the sand running as she looked at me and said, "Ah . . . Charles, room eight is available."

Except for mine, she had a remarkable memory for names. She laughed and joked with most of her customers and even remembered what part of England Allan came from.

The establishment of American House came about by accident. A couple of young hookers had fallen in love with two soldiers who were stationed at San Diego. When the soldiers were transferred to Edmonton, the hookers came along to be near their lovers. Their first weekend in Edmonton, they plied their trade on Jasper Avenue, the main street of the city, did a brisk business, but were soon hustled off to jail by the city's highly efficient morality detectives. They were remanded in custody for seven days after having blood samples taken to determine whether or not they were infected with VD. The results were negative, the girls were treated as first offenders and released on the understanding that they would leave the city immediately. The morality detectives suggested that the girls give Calgary, Alberta's other major city two hundred miles to the south, a try, stating that there were more heathens there, and that Calgary didn't enforce their laws against prostitution as stringently as did Edmonton.

Instead of leaving town, the girls answered Mrs. B's ad for easy money and short hours, and were soon ensconced in one of Mrs. B's upstairs rooms, studying the sales procedures of Corsetina Corsets.

"They sold damn few corsets," Mrs. B would say, retelling the story any time anyone asked how she had got involved in "the business." "But they sure had a lot of prospective customers dropping in," and she would laugh her gruff laugh and light one Sweet Caporal from the butt of another.

It didn't take Mrs. B long to guess what was going on, and she soon confronted the girls not only to confirm her suspicions, but to get details of the financial intricacies of the business, for Mrs. B was never one to miss a business opportunity. Rather than turn the girls out on the street again, she simply upped their rent 500 percent, which they gladly paid. The girls promptly wrote to two friends in San Diego explaining the potential in Edmonton, and American House was born.

After that, whenever a girl came to apply for a job selling Corsetina Corsets, she was interviewed not only by Mrs. B, but often by two or more of the working girls, who were soon able to establish if the newcomer had any previous experience with prostitution, or the temperament and inclination to make a success of it as an occupation.

Edmonton was still really a small town, or at least had a small-town mentality, and rumors of the existence of American House were soon rampant in the city. My father took me aside one Sunday evening when I was allowed off base, ostensibly to warn me of the unsavory aspects of prostitution, but more realistically, to find out the exact location of American House. I really doubt that he wanted the information for his own use, but being an inveterate storyteller, I'm sure he wanted to impress his friends with his knowledge.

Much to my embarrassment, he kept pressing to know if I'd been there. He put his arm around my shoulder and was so close I could smell his Aqua-Velva, and tried some of that phony father-son camaraderie that made him sound and act like a carnival barker, with me as the prize rube.

For some reason, I found the situation intolerably funny and had to clench my teeth, bite my tongue and the insides of my mouth, to keep from breaking down in laughter. It was so plain what my father wanted, but he didn't have the guts to come right out and ask me to tell him the location of American House. I barely listened to him as he talked to me like a five-year-old, lecturing about the evils of venereal disease and the immorality of prostitution.

As Mrs. B's entourage grew, it became necessary to have someone to control the traffic, as it were, and Mrs. B was the obvious choice. It was her idea to use the hourglasses to control the amount of time a customer could spend with the girl of his choice. Mrs. B ended up having eight to ten girls in the house at all times. American House had someone on duty from ten A.M. to two A.M. to accommodate all three shifts from the military bases as well as the nearby aircraft manufacturing plant.

About a month after American House became fully established, a bluenosed neighbor, noticing the unusual amount of activity flourishing around Mrs. B's day and night, alerted the local police force and early one Saturday evening a lugubrious black paddy wagon pulled up in front and a dozen of Edmonton's finest raided American House. They marched out of the house, Mrs. B fully clothed, and eight girls in various stages of undress. They took them to the police station where the girls were booked as inmates of a bawdy house and Mrs. B as the keeper. It did not take long for word of the arrests to reach the powers that be among the American military.

The legend is that a certain lieutenant colonel who was not getting any glory out of overseeing the movement of supplies and troops to Alaska, and was also a regular customer of American House, dressed in his full battle regalia with three aides-de-camp, a military limousine, and a convoy of jeeps, sped through the dark streets of Edmonton that Saturday night and parked outside the police station. He and his whole contingent are reported to have waited patiently until the chief of police was roused from bed and summoned to his office.

Exactly what went on in the office of the chief of police is not known, but again legend takes over. The lieutenant colonel is supposed to have told the chief that there were five thousand American troops in Edmonton and another two to three thousand who could be summoned on short notice, and that unless Mrs. B and her girls were released immediately and given safe conduct for the duration of the lieutenant colonel's stay in Edmonton, he was about to issue weekend passes to every American soldier in Edmonton including all of the military police, and he hoped that the Edmonton police chief was prepared to handle five to seven thousand unsupervised American soldiers, drunk, horny and spoiling for trouble.

The result was that later that day Mrs. B and her women were returned to American House, not by paddy wagon or police car, but in the chief's private limousine.

Mrs. B and American House received no further harassment and the lieutenant colonel often posted an MP just inside the back door of American House to insure that a certain decorum was maintained. But even without supervision, GIs of both armies knew a good thing when they had it, and there was seldom anything worse than a soldier passing out in the hall and eventually being carried back to base by his buddies.

"Room eight is free," she said to me, motioning Allan to stay behind in the parlor. "We'll have a girl for you in a minute, Sonny," she said, nodding toward the pink sand that was already rapidly disappearing from the No. 4 hourglass.

The light in the upstairs hall came from a tiny flickering twenty-watt bulb with a poinsettia-colored filament. The hall smelled of linoleum, floor wax and mothballs.

I tapped on the dark varnished door which had an equally dark metal No. 8 nailed to it, and entered. The girl stood with her back to me looking out the room's only window at the snow-deep front yard. She didn't turn around although she obviously knew I was there.

After a brief silence, I said, "My name is Charles." There followed a longer silence. She wore a dress of green silky material. Her hair was a mouse-brown and pulled into a bun at the back of her head. She was quite short and stocky.

"I'm sorry to bother you," I said finally, "but Mrs. B thought you were expecting me."

She turned around and looked in my direction. She was not pretty. The brightness of her dress contrasted vividly with the dark varnished windowsill, baseboards, trim around the closet, and the grayish color of the walls. Her nose was too large, her lips too thick, and she didn't have much of a chest. There were tears on her cheeks.

"I'm Theodozia," she said, putting out a very small hand for me to shake. A peculiar gesture under the circumstances.

"I'm Charles Bristow," I said, for want of something better to say.

"They call me Teddy," said the girl. "My last name is Czorokovitch. I come from out around Smokey Lake."

This was not going the way it was supposed to. Why, I wondered, did this type of thing always seem to happen to me?

"I'm sorry," Teddy said, "I just found out something I didn't know." She sniffed. Then she took a step toward me and laid her cheek against my chest. "Helen just told me I got a baby in me. I didn't know . . . I didn't know that this was . . . the way you got one. I just didn't know." She sobbed into my chest like a brokenhearted child.

Teddy was, I suppose, no more than eighteen and spoke with a heavy Ukrainian accent, where *h*'s are silent and *e*'s pronounced as a heavy *a*. Thus Edmonton became Aadmonton, and Teddy, Taaddy.

"You must think that's awful funny," she said into my chest, "that something like that could happen . . . that somebody could be so stupid."

"I haven't really thought about it," I said into the top of her head, but I was thinking about it, and my mind flashed to my own nonexistent sex education, and I saw how it very well could happen. I had heard of girls asking if they could get pregnant by kissing and women who didn't know they were pregnant until their baby was born.

"I don't come from around here," Teddy said, as if that explained her ignorance. "Used to live out near Spedden." She pronounced it Spaaden. I knew vaguely where it was, a tiny farming community one hundred miles or so northeast of Edmonton. "But, you don't want to know my trouble," she said, stepping back and extracting a crumpled handkerchief from the sleeve of her dress. As she blew her nose she looked sadly up at me. If she had been wearing glasses she would have been looking over the top of them.

I felt an incredible rush of tenderness toward this bedraggled girl, but could find no way of expressing myself. I was afraid that if I showed the compassion I felt, I would become ridiculous in her eyes, after all she was a prostitute, she was infinitely more experienced with life than me, and yet . . .

"Why don't we just talk for a while," I said.

Teddy let out an audible sigh and moved over to the bed. We lay facing each other on our elbows on the worn, wheat-colored bedspread. Teddy lit a cigarette and set the sardine-can ashtray on the bed behind her.

"I was feeling bad anyway because my parents come to visit me this afternoon," she said. She was so plain and ordinary, I somehow couldn't reconcile myself to where I was. It didn't seem possible that Mrs. B and her hourglasses were just one flight down and that the other rooms were in use. "My mother's a dummy. Did I tell you that? That's maybe why she never told me nothing about . . . you know. I didn't speak no English until I start school and then I was always a grade or two behind everyone else."

I reached across and took her free hand and squeezed it gently.

"Hey, you're nice to listen to me this way. Most guys would have got mad at me by now."

"It's okay," I said and smiled at her. I tried to picture what my life would be like with Teddy. What if I took her away from this life, gave her and the baby a good home. I would read aloud to her in the evenings . . .

"My old man phoned from the bus depot, Mrs. B took the call. She's real nice, said it would be okay for them to come over. I told Papa to take a taxi but they walked. Got to be close to two miles. There's no business on a weekday afternoon, so it was just like they was coming to a regular rooming house. Not that they'd know. Anyway, I was getting the room cleaned up when I got talking to Helen . . ." Her voice trailed off. She leaned back and put the cigarette out, then as if there was some prearranged signal, we both lay down, me on my back and Teddy with her head in the crook of my neck.

"I just got talking to Helen," she waved her hand to show Helen was one of her housemates, "and I was telling her about how I been sick every morning, throw up sick to die, and she asks me how long since I had a period and I didn't even know what she's talking about. She have to say, 'When did you bleed last?' before I know. And I tell her it's been maybe three months. I was happy when it stopped. It was always so much of a mess." She pulled back and looked at me again as if she was wearing glasses and gave me a small smile.

" 'Jesus, kid, don't you know nothing?' Helen says to me. 'You're knocked up, pregnant, got a bun in the oven.' I don't know what to say to her. I just feel all of a sudden all heavy inside like my stomach is full of rocks or something. I come back here and go through the effort of clean up my room and wait for my folks to come."

Teddy got up then, climbed over me, her slippery green dress climbing way up over her knees, but she didn't seem to notice. She just walked over to the window and pulled back the cream-colored lace curtains.

"If you look out the window here in the daytime, you can see quite a ways down the street. I seen them coming and washed my face and blew my nose before they got here."

I could picture Teddy's father and mother. I had seen their prototypes blocking the aisles of the T. Eaton Department Store all the years of my life. The father in a dark red or green plaid hunting hat with ear-flaps down, walking a full five paces ahead of his woman. He would be wearing bib overalls with a denim smock over a bulky sweater. The mother would be wearing a heavy brown or black coat over a black dress that hung below the coat. She would be short and heavy with round red cheeks and her head covered with a flowered babushka. On their feet each would be wearing full-shoe rubbers stuffed with insoles and held on by sealer rings of white or orangey-red.

"Mrs. B let them in and showed them up here to my room just like they was a trick or something," and she made a weak little smile. "I hug Mama and her face is all cold from the outside and both their clothes smell of wood smoke, and Papa's mackinaw have the sweet smells of clover hay and cows hanging on it like pictures. I'd almost forgot what it was like to live way out there. No gas, or power, or water.

"They'd been to the Army & Navy Department Store, Mama is carrying two shopping bags and Papa got a square kind of package look like a blanket. We ain't got nothing to say to each other. I asked about my brother. He stayed home to do the farm chores, and they asked about my job . . . I tell them I sell corsets door to door. I have to bring out samples to show them what corsets are. Papa laugh some and say how come they want to make nice fat women look like they are slim, and he pat Mama's back. She's all round and her tummy jiggles when she walks. They believe it about my job, I guess. They got no reason not to. Mrs. B make a point of telling them how well I'm doing. They both smile and say they're glad I'm doing so good in the city.

"Mrs. B brings them up a cup of tea and then they go. As they was leaving Mama dug down in her shopping bag and she give me that there picture on the dresser."

I have to turn my head to see the picture. It is a picture of the Virgin. It is in a pale wood frame and probably sold for thirty-five cents. The colors are a kaleidoscope of sky blues, canary yellows, vermilions, and Kelly greens.

Nowadays, my son has a word for such pictures. Clone Art, he calls them, although he includes in that definition almost any nonprofessional artwork found in ordinary homes or offices. I doubt if there was such a word as "clone" in 1943.

"It's very nice," I said, not knowing what else to say.

"Yeah," said Teddy. She seemed to be feeling a little better. "It makes me sad to fool them like that."

"It's better than telling them the truth though, isn't it?"

"I suppose," she said and sat down glumly on the room's only chair.

"How? How did you . . . ?"

"Get to working here? By accident, I guess. Everything was by accident. I don't know how I could ever be so dumb. I just never thought . . . until Helen told me . . ." She sniffed loudly again.

"Things will be all right," I said.

"When I was fourteen or so boys got to looking pretty good to me. Guy name of John Repchuck take me out one night in his pickup truck. He kiss me a lot and put his hands all over me, and it feel so good I let him do whatever he want with me and that feel good too. I start to go out with some of his friends after that. I sure liked being so popular, but I never catch on that I bet I'm the only girl who does it with every guy every time she goes out. It just seem to me that anything that feel so good can't be bad for me."

"Did you know what to expect when you came to . . . work . . . here?"

"I really applied for a job to sell things, but a couple of the girls explain to me what really happens here. Jesus, but I was surprised to find out from Mrs. B that I could get paid money for doing what I like to do best. Still, the other girls act like they doing something dirty and it rub off on me sometimes, like today when Mama gave me that picture."

I glanced back at the peacock-colored Virgin leaning gaudily against the mirror as Teddy, or a counterpart, might lean on a lamppost. Teddy looked at me and smiled. She was really prettier when she smiled. Her teeth were uneven, but then who was perfect. I pictured myself standing at the end of a church aisle glancing furtively over my shoulder as Teddy, dressed in a white wedding gown, advanced slowly down the aisle toward me.

"We'd better get on with it," Teddy said standing up. "Your time will be up soon." Her face was still splotched and red from crying.

"It's all right," I said, standing helplessly in the middle of the room. She took one step toward me, then rushed the other step or two while the beginning of a colossal sob forced itself from her. She buried her face in my chest and sobbed uncontrollably. "You're so nice to me," I think were the words that came choking out between sobs.

"There, there," I said, patting her pale brown hair that was escaping bit by bit from the bun at the back of her neck.

She took a deep breath. "No. You paid your money. It's not fair." She took a step back, reached down and took my hand to lead me to the bed. I sat on the edge of the bed. She took another deep breath and sniffed loudly. This was certainly not going to be one of the most passionate experiences of my life. Teddy reached out her arms and clasped them behind my neck and was just leaning forward to kiss me when I felt her tense as if a gun had suddenly been poked into her back. She unclasped her hands, stood up and walked the two or three steps to the dresser.

She took the picture of the Virgin from where it leaned, solemnly staring at us in all its garish wonder, and turned it toward the wall.

"I don't want she should see the things I do," Teddy said to me.

Seconds later Mrs. B knocked and called, "Time."

"I'll see you again soon," I said as I left, feeling very pleased with myself. Teddy gave me a demure kiss on the lips and squeezed my hand.

"That would be very nice," she said. I closed the door quietly.

When I came downstairs Allan was waiting for me, the lemony-blond hair on either side of his beret freshly watered. With him were two young American soldiers about our age. One was tall with sharp features and very black hair, the other stocky with curly red hair and freckles piled on his cheeks like cornflakes.

"Well, it took you long enough," said Allan.

I tried to smile enigmatically. What was the quote from *A Tale of Two Cities*? " 'Tis a far far better thing I do than ever I have done before." I looked at the Americans in their tailored uniforms. Allan and I looked like poor relatives in our fuzzy khaki and the hateful black berets.

"So, you must have given your woman quite a workout," the tallest of the two Americans said to me as we walked down the frozen wooden sidewalks in the direction of our barracks. He had very dark eyes and wore a great deal of after-shave lotion. His voice had an unusual softness, at least to my ear.

"Yes, tell us about it, Charles," Allan said.

"Which one were you with?" asked the redhead.

I could feel myself blushing furiously. I kicked at the sidewalk as we walked along. Some of the houses we passed had red Christmas candles in their windows although it was well past the traditional Christmas date. A large number of Edmontonians of Slavic descent celebrated Christmas by the

Gregorian calendar. I pictured Teddy with a creamy lace prayer shawl bunched about her face. The whole city was covered in a light hoar frost.

"Come on, Charles," Allan insisted. "Who were you with?"

I stepped sharply on the outside edge of the wooden sidewalk. A nail cried out in the cold like a kicked animal.

"Theodozia," I said very quietly.

"Who?" said the tall American.

I decided to keep on being mysterious. "Theodozia Czorokovitch," I said. The name had kind of a mysterious sound to it. It sounded like the name of a heroine in a silent movie.

"No such," said the red-haired American. "I know every girl there."

"His daddy owns a brewery," said the tall one of the redhead. "Sends him money every week for him to spend all on himself." His voice was breathy and for some reason reminded me of a freshly waxed floor.

I felt like a treed animal being slowly set up for the kill. My stomach lurched the way it does when an elevator stops suddenly. Something was terribly wrong.

"Teddy," sang the short one.

"Teddy," the other two echoed. "You got stuck with Teddy."

"Stuck," I echoed stupidly.

"That's why he was gone so long."

"He was listening instead of fucking."

"Did she talk you out of it entirely, or just . . ."

"Which story did she use on you?"

"The visit from her parents?"

"Or the sick baby sister."

"Her mother has TB?"

"Or the stepfather who sold her to Mrs. B."

"I don't know what you mean," I said lamely. Why did everyone in the world but me know what was going on?

"She talked you right out of it, didn't she?" said Allan, walking backward in front of me, doing a little dance.

"No," I said. "It wasn't . . ." It couldn't be. The picture of the Virgin. Her parents *were* there.

"She did too," said Allan.

"Old Teddy's tried to hustle every guy who's ever been with her," said the redhead. "Blake here caught right on and slapped her around some. Said she was the best fuck he ever had after they got that straightened out." He looked to Blake for confirmation.

"I been back to her," said Blake. "When she sees it's me, she just drops the laundry and spreads her legs. She can be a mighty sweet fuck when she wants to be."

"She wants to be an actress," said the redhead.

"She is," said Allan.

The chill January wind suddenly penetrated my uniform and I felt as cold as if I were clothed in the hoar frost that covered the trees, utility poles and wires. I walked rapidly ahead of them beating my hands on alternate shoulders. I looked up at a frosty streetlight and I could see Teddy's face, her green dress, the picture of the Virgin. Soon the taunting voices were far behind me, and there was only the cold and the stars and the sounds of my feet on the frozen sidewalks.

The
Blacksmith
Shop Caper

*O*ctober 15.
A brown envelope arrived in the morning mail containing, in federal government paraphrase, the seven words which strike the most fear into the heart of a freelance writer: your unemployment money has been cut off.

Alternatives: drive taxi, cook pizza, write for money.

Have at various times engaged in all three. Vehicular transportation of vomiting drunks and sick old ladies no longer excites me, neither does sweating in a 250° kitchen with tomato sauce up to my armpits.

Occasionally, when desperate, freelance for a triweekly scandal sheet cum newspaper. Have heard rumors that their new editor is an old friend. He is indeed, but I would never have known it by the name plaque on his desk, which reads Kenneth Bromley.

Bromley: Twenty years ago we attended school together in a frigid prairie city. His name then was Kazimer Borowski. His old man worked on the killing floor at Swift's Packing Plant. Was drunk every Friday. About ten P.M. would single-handedly take on the twelve Poles who comprised the afternoon shift at Townley's Tire Town across the street from the Railroad Hotel. He lost. Always. Every Friday midnight could be found sleeping on the gravel in alley behind Tire Town. Kazimer and I would load him in Kazimer's *Iron Duke* wagon and take turns pulling him home.

Explain to Kazimer/Kenneth that publisher is a personal friend and that the ex-editor gave me assignments. I have never met the publisher, but my bluff worked on the former editor. K/K looks harassed, digs into desk, offers me choice between interview with a party-hopping politician and an analysis of school board policies.

Detest article writing. It requires close adherence to facts, often entails research. I prefer to invent facts. Politician has the IQ of a shoe, a rented dog, a rich wife, more followers than Hitler. Bromley says general tone of interview should be favorable. Promise I will disclose that politician has bed-wetting problem. Offer withdrawn. Would rather starve than write about school boards.

Consider giving up. Then look more closely at Bromley. Kazimer is no longer Ukrainian: wears a tweed suit, horn-rimmed glasses, speaks with a definite British accent. May have had a nose job. Often says, "Old Fellow." Occasional, "By Jove!" Appears to believe he has become Anglo-Saxon. Publisher is British. Osmosis is a wonderful thing.

"Does your boss know you're Ukrainian?"

"Old Fellow, you wouldn't."

"Not if I get an assignment with expenses."

Leave moments later with fifty dollars clutched to my heart, assigned to write five-thousand-word profile on the cabaret scene in our city from point of view of single person. Lied about being single. Would precipitate World War III for fifty dollars. Bromley wants, in his words, "a new-journalism approach," observations on general scene, specifics on my experiences. For fifty bucks I am expected to score.

On the way home, spent twenty-five dollars on groceries. Hesitantly tell wife of assignment. She volunteers to accompany me.

"I'll screen the applicants," she says cynically.

Remind her that story is to be written from single viewpoint. She shrugs. "Would you like a meal when you get home?"

"Aren't you worried?"

"About what? You couldn't pick up a suitcase."

Gravely insulted. Retire to contemplate past triumphs.

1) Girl in pink cashmere sweater in ninth grade social studies class: lewd conduct behind map of Eurasia.

2) High school: best friend's sister in back of best friend's father's Oldsmobile, parked in garage that smelled of cedar shavings and used Johnny Cat.

3) First love: waited impatiently for three months for her parents to go to IOOF Christmas party. Got her down to panties and socks before she thought she heard a car in the driveway and hid me in a closet.

4) Ex-wife.

5) Ex-wife's mother.

6) Girl with long nails who picked me up in a coffee shop. Had just had a furious fight with husband concerning his alleged infidelity. Anxious for revenge. Thirty-six hours of nonstop revenge. Happy to send her back to husband who must have more scar tissue than Evel Knievel.

7) Present wife: super-cool lady who paid for the motel on our second date. Is usually right.

I have never picked up a girl.

Prepare carefully for expedition. Wear one and only pair of dress pants. Daughter calls them floaters. Something about them being too short. She also makes fun of my good shoes which I last wore to a funeral in 1976. Consider putting shoe polish on gray hairs in beard and moustache. Try to look younger. Will collapse if some girl refers to me as Pops. Have to reluctantly admit that I may not be perfect for the assignment. Loathe dancing. Have conversational ability of watercress. Still thinking of devastating replies to put-downs suffered in high school.

Last minute review of book, *How to Pick Up Girls:* given to me by wife as a joke. What do you say to a girl in a supermarket? Pardon me, miss, do you know where they keep the canned antelope? Brush up on section dealing with singles' bars.

Have a change of heart at the last moment. Decide to take along a distant friend. Howard has been suggesting for years that we go out chasing girls. Claims he is good at it. He has a cheerful little wife about a hundred pounds overweight, three faucet-nosed children, the youngest of whom lies under the sofa and snarls at visitors. Howard rewinds lawn mower motors for a living. Not reputed to be a swinger.

Tells his wife that I need to borrow him for unnamed research project. "What kind?" she wants to know.

"Have been assigned to count streetlights in downtown area," I tell her. She buys it. Smiles, jiggling several of her chins, asks Howard if he wants a meal when he gets home. She would have believed Chicken Little.

Howard is shorter, older, has less hair, wears thicker glasses and his clothing is more out of style than mine. Howard is also sneakier. He insists on taking his car, which is full of crayons, Lego and orange peels. But while I drive, again at Howard's insistence, he produces from a secret compartment under the back seat a Johnny Carson jacket, Johnny Miller slacks, a pair of Dingos, a Garo Yepremian tie, contact lenses, a bottle of Brut and a wig that makes him look like Mac Davis.

"I play cards with the boys every Thursday night," he says with a leer, nudging me in the ribs and winking. He assures me he is really good at picking up girls.

I planned to go to a dope and denim cabaret: cheap, informal, a couple of fights for entertainment. Howard turns out to be a snob. Only the best cabaret in town for him. Place has a two-dollar cover charge. I consider cover charges a close relative of pay toilets and parking garages. Refuse to indulge in them because I like to get something tangible for my money. I allow Howard to pay cover charge. No need for him to know I am on expenses.

Cabaret is called the Blacksmith Shop. Walls adorned with work objects such as rakes, hoes and tongs of various sizes, along with many photographs of workmen from early 1900s. Nostalgia is a strange disease, the naming of cabarets even stranger. Any place that ordinary people wouldn't be found drowned is a good name for a cabaret. Band playing "Sweet Caroline." Was last here four years ago, they were playing "Sweet Caroline" then. Can hardly wait for "Raindrops Keep Falling on My Head," vocalist sings it while holding an umbrella. Last time here got indecently drunk. Made a pass at best friend's wife. May have been successful. Have not seen best friend for four years.

Order a Graveyard Smasher: double dark rum, half Coke, half orange juice. Three, and you're out tipping over tombstones. Howard and I sit at a table for two. Howard has a view of the cabaret. I have a view of Howard and a wall. Cabaret is about two acres, large enough to graze buffalo. Dance floor at center shimmers like a swimming pool.

Howard asks first girl he sees to dance. I stare at the wall. Howard returns, admonishes me for not dancing. I bare my teeth at him, consider pulling off his wig and running. Howard reminds me of a tennis player between games: he takes a swig of his drink, wipes his forehead with a handkerchief and marches back to the wars. I move to Howard's chair and look around. Couples seem to sit mainly in one area. Appears to be an unwritten rule that single guys do not venture into that area looking for dancing partners, although it is all right for a guy with a date to ask another guy's date to dance. Singles sit in separate area. Females invariably come in twos and fours. Likewise guys. Socializing difficult. Tables seat two and four.

To my right a table of jocks grunt to each other, occasionally beat chests. Probably rugby players. Could all act in remake of bar scene from *Star Wars* without makeup. Insist on having beer bottles delivered to table unopened so they can bite off caps and necks with much braying. Three out of four appear to be toilet trained. May not be rugby players after all.

Nearby a table of military types. Enough hair for one person divided among four. Each walks like he has a bayonet against the small of his back. Already fighting among themselves. Predict at least one will barf on the carpet before evening is over. Hope we remain a neutral country. These guys couldn't stand guard over a vacant lot.

Off to the left, a redhead and her girlfriend. Long hair the color of ground red pepper, green eyes, just enough freckles to make her desirable. Have always been partial to redheads. Can't see girlfriend clearly, but from the back she resembles a Volkswagen. Consider asking redhead to dance. Try to think of something interesting to say to her. Try to think of anything to say to her. Reconsider. Will have another drink first.

Bandleader announces in a nasal lisp that next dance is ladies' choice. Thought ladies' choice went out with sock hops and Patti Page records. Bandleader's sideburns disappear into collar, has nose large enough to enter an Olympic competition. Looks like the kind of guy who could follow you into a revolving door and come out ahead of you.

Here comes the redhead! I smile. Try desperately to look like James Caan. She walks right by me, asks one of the jocks to dance. Hope he doesn't break any of her feet with his knuckles. Feel tap on my shoulder. Tall, dark lady in red dress asks me to dance. Can tell by the way she walks toward the dance floor that she is quite drunk. Music too loud to converse. Walks me back to table, asks if I'm alone. I nod. She sits down, signals waitress for drinks. I pay. Her name is Lawanda. She was probably pretty when she was sixteen.

Tells me her life story in five minutes. Needless to say, she hasn't had much of a life. Her boyfriend works at the bar.

Name is Jack. He takes her for granted. She has to do his laundry on her day off. Lawanda is about thirty-five, brown eyes, very wide mouth, looks like she has endured a long succession of alcoholic boyfriends and repossessed furniture. She is a toucher. Her hands are cold and at least ten years older than she is. Keeps apologizing for being drunk. Keeps saying it is time for her to go home because she has to be at work at eight A.M. Is obviously waiting for me to offer her a ride. Intimates with very little subtlety that it may be worth my while. As ladies go, Lawanda has about a hundred thousand miles on her.

Excuse myself and go to washroom. Stay for twenty minutes. Lean against wall. Pretend to dry hands on paper towel. Easy to tell who has a date. Singles use massive amounts of breath spray, Certs, Clorets, after-shave. Occasional can of aerosol underarm spray appears to provide a couple of fast blasts under jacket. Guys with dates do their business and depart. Singles comb hair in as many as three different styles. The less hair, the more combing.

Check out cubicles. Very indifferent graffiti. *Sandra sucks cocks,* followed by a phone number. Have no pen. Commit it to memory. Wonder if anybody ever phones those numbers?

Peek out door. Coast appears to be clear. Decide to make tour of cabaret. Haven't seen Howard in over an hour. Notice Lawanda hovering nearby, pretend not to see her. Music is much louder. Dance floor looks like an aquarium full of frightened fish. Have never been able to grasp rationale of dancing. There must be an easier way to get to touch girls. Find it difficult to believe that anyone actually enjoys it. Being born with a tin ear and the coordination of a forklift may have something to do with my attitude.

Spot Howard in a booth with three girls. He is sitting between two, one is opposite him. All are laughing and talking animatedly. Quick appraisal. Two above average, one doggie. Guess which side of the table she is on?

The doggie must have a death wish to go out looking as she does. Is in dire need of electrolysis due to terminal case of five o'clock shadow. Howard introduces me. Shake my head in amazement when I discover what the conversation is about. They are showing each other pictures of their children. Howard is waving some color photos of his brats. Instead of strafing him with swizzle sticks for insulting their intelligence, the girls match him picture for picture. To me his companions look about nineteen. One of them has a kid in third grade. I am getting old.

Howard excuses himself. Whispers to me that he has action going in three parts of the cabaret, has to check on his other interests. It must be hell to have to spread yourself so thin. The booth is suddenly very quiet. I tend to have that effect on groups. Music is at jungle intensity. Girls across from me are bouncing up and down on upholstery. Why not? Tomorrow morning they will be rinsing diapers in the toilet bowl. Thankfully, military types stagger by and ask girls to dance. Doggie and I are left alone. I have forgotten her name. She is the type of girl whose mother probably forgets her name. I look at her. She looks at me. Silence. Eventually, she excuses herself. Will probably stay in washroom for twenty minutes to make certain I am gone. I will be.

Tour remainder of cabaret. Happy party of eight ensconced in far corner. Among that group Kenneth Bromley and his bride. Make a point of almost calling him Kazimer. He cringes, neglects to invite me to join them. I do anyway. Graveyard Smashers finally beginning to take their toll. I tell twenty-five Ukrainian jokes each one more vile than the last. Anyone named Kenneth Bromley has to laugh at Ukrainian jokes. Observe his wife carefully. Can it be that she does not know? If I am here on assignment why am I still alone, Bromley hisses at me.

As an answer, I whisk Mrs. Bromley off to the dance floor. Keep her there for three sets. Let Kazimer squirm. She is a very pleasant little blonde with several tiers of even white teeth. Find out from her that Kenneth was born in England. Orphaned at an early age. It is midnight. Wonder if old Nestor Borowski is sleeping in alley in frigid prairie city. Return bride to table. Give Bromley a smile that says, you and I know that I'm going to be working quite steadily from now on. Order round of drinks. Point out Bromley as payor.

Feeling so good, I venture across cabaret to ask redhead to dance, barely avoiding Lawanda. Quickly review technique for picking up girls. Advice works well if you're not a coward. Catch 22: if you're not a coward, you don't need the advice.

Music very slow. Hold redhead close. May be in love.

"You're a very attractive lady. I have always been partial to redheads."

"Yeah, I seen youse lookin' at me a while back."

She has a voice like fingernails on a blackboard. Quickly fall out of love. Feel like a pile of inner tubes.

Deposit redhead. Cruise some more. Note Howard groping with large-bosomed blonde in peach-colored semiformal. Hope they don't get their wigs locked.

Lawanda collars me with her cold fingers. We dance. As the number ends, spot back of very familiar head among fish. Know now how Cortez felt when he discovered whatever it was he discovered.

"Pardon me, miss, can you tell me where they keep the canned antelope?"

"I was right. You couldn't pick up a suitcase." Tempted to make bad pun about bags. Resist temptation. Introduce Lawanda to wife. Lawanda releases my arm, scuttles away.

Unfortunately, my wife is accompanied by Howard's wife. We have to pass Howard's booth in order to get to the girls' table. Try to get between Mrs. Howard and the booth. No need. She looks right at him, doesn't recognize Howard in wig and wild threads. Howard buries head in voluptuous blond bosom as we pass. Mrs. Howard is wearing black satin tent festooned with red shooting stars: straight out of a

Rousseau. Howard is out the door by the time we get to the girls' table. Explain that he was not feeling well, left some time ago.

Last dance. Hold wife close, give K/K the high sign behind her back. He gives me a fifty-dollar smile. Linger at door to gather last impressions. Most who came alone go home alone. Hold on to wife and Mrs. Howard. Wink at ugliest jock as he crawls to sidewalk on all fours. He ignores me. Is already asking a parking meter if it lives alone.

First Names
and
Empty Pockets

A doll is a witness
who cannot die
with a doll you are never alone.
— Margaret Atwood

*F*act, fiction, fantasy, folk-lore, swirl in a haze of color, like a hammer-thrower tossing a rainbow. And always, I am haunted by images of broken dolls. Old dolls, lying, arms and legs askew, as if dropped from a great height; dolls with painted, staring eyes, faces full of eggshell cracks, powdered with dust, smelling of abandonment.

JOPLIN TOPS CHARTS!
SPLASHERS MAKE A SPLASH!

The headlines are from *Billboard* and *Cashbox*, publications which have become my main reading fare over the past two decades. We've been married for nearly fifteen years, Janis and I. *Splashers* is her seventeenth album.

The idea for the album cover was mine: Janis seated side-saddle on a chromed Harley. Two views: one, she is facing the camera, her carrot-colored hair below her shoulders, less frizzed, but wild and windblown as always; she is wearing jeans, pale blue platform shoes, rhinestones embedded in the crisscross straps that disappear under her cuffs, a denim jacket, open, showing a white T-shirt with SPLASHERS! in bold red capitals. She looks scarcely a day older than when I met her. The cosmetics of the years, the lines around the corners of her mouth, eyes, and at the bridge of her nose, have been air-brushed away and she grins, eyes flashing. She is smoking a cigarette, looking tough and sexy.

The flip side of the album features Janis's back and spotlights the cycle-gang colors: a golden patch on the faded denim in the shape of a guitar, again with the word *Splashers* only this time in black script.

Before I discovered Janis my life was peopled by antiseptic women with short hair and cool dresses, sexless as dolls. Always they lurk like ghosts just out of my vision. I smell their coolness, hear their measured voices, see their shapes when I close my eyes. I shudder them away and think of Janis crooning her love for me alone, our bodies tangled and wet. I think of her and of our mouths overflowing with the taste of each other, and I recall the San Francisco street where I first told her my name. My whole name.

"Man, you got something nobody else on the street has."

"Huh?"

"A last name, man. Around here it's all first names and empty pockets. Beer and hard times. Watching the streets turn blue at four A.M. while you cadge quarters at a bus stop or outside a bar. Do they have freaky chicks like me where you come from?"

Also, on the back of the album, there is an inset photo of the band, Saturday Night Swindle. *Splashers* is their sixth album with us. It was my idea to change bands—Big Brother and the Holding Company were never much—but Janis started with them and we stuck with them for eleven albums.

"This is what I do instead of having kids," Janis jokes. And it is true that she has averaged an album every nine months for nearly ten years.

I know little about music, even after all these years. *Janis* is my job, my life. "Like holding a lid on a pressure cooker with bare hands," is how I described my life with Janis to *Time* magazine, the last time they did a cover story. Generally, I trust the judgment of record producers when it comes to music, though recording the Tanya Tucker song "What's Your Mama's Name?" was my idea. The album, our unlucky thirteenth, has sold nearly two million. I chose the musicians for Saturday Night Swindle. I had an agent I trusted send me resumés of five musicians for each position. Musically there was little to choose, but I had their backgrounds investigated and chose with endurance in mind. There are no heavy drinkers and no hard drug users in this band. The less temptation available the better.

While they were photographing Janis for the album cover, redoing the front scene for the twentieth time, I crossed the set to her, knelt down and turned up the left cuff of her jeans about three one-inch turns: the way you see it on the album cover.

"What the fuck are you doing?" Janis demanded.

"It's just a touch. It's the way you were when we first met. Do you remember?"

"Nah. My memory don't go that far back. That's all ancient fucking history."

I raise my head and look at her. She grins and her eyes tell me that she does indeed remember.

I straighten up. "I'd kiss you, but the makeup man would hemorrhage."

"Later, Sugar," and she purses her lips in an imitation kiss. One of the photographers looks quizzically at the rolled-up denim and then at me.

"Trust me," I say.

She sidled up to me, plump, wide-waisted, a sunset of hair in a frizzy rainbow around her face. Her hand hooked at the sleeve of my jacket.

"Looking for a girl?"

"How much?" There was a long pause as if she was genuinely surprised that I was interested. Her eyes flashed on my face, instantly retreated to the sidewalk. Then she uttered a single, almost inaudible word, like a solitary note of music that hung in the silence of the soft San Francisco night.

"Five."

I almost laughed it was so pitiful. Would have if she had resembled the whores I'd seen downtown: booted, bra-less, hard as bullets, whores who asked for thirty dollars, sometimes forty dollars, plus the room. I took a quick look at her, a husky, big-boned girl with a wide face and squarish jaw, anything but pretty, but I found her appealing, vulnerable, in need.

There was another long pause before I said, "Okay." Her fingers still gripped the sleeve of my jacket. We were on a dark street a mile or more from downtown San Francisco, a street full of ghostly old houses and occasional small shops. The houses were three-storey, some with balconies, all with latticework, and cast eerie shadows over the street. It was my first of three days in San Francisco. I had never been there before.

"Where do we go?" she said and looked around the deserted street as if hoping that a hotel might suddenly materialize.

"I'm a stranger here," I said. "I thought you'd know of a place."

"Yeah, well I'm kind of lost myself. Just got to walking. I don't usually leave the downtown. Business hasn't been very good tonight," and she made an effort at a smile. She was wearing faded jeans, one cuff rolled up about four inches as if she had recently ridden a bicycle.

The Iowa town where I come from, where I've lived all my life, is a white-siding and verandah town of twenty thousand souls, of old but newly painted houses on tree-lined streets, lilacs, American flags, one-pump service stations, and good neighbors.

I work framing buildings, sawing, pounding nails, bare to the waist in the humid summers, bronzed as maple, sweat blinding my eyes, my hands scarred. I will likely never leave this town except for a brief holiday to San Francisco, and possibly a honeymoon trip; later, we will take our daughters to Disneyland.

The house where I live with my parents is square and white, so perfect it might have been built with a child's blocks. There are marigolds, asters and bachelor buttons growing in a kaleidoscope of color between the sidewalk and the soft, manicured lawn. On a porch pillar, just above the black metal mailbox, is a sign, black on white, about a foot square that reads: DOLL HOSPITAL.

In my workshop I make dolls as well as repair them. I show them to no one for they are always incomplete. Broken dolls: fat pink arms that end at shredded wrists, sightless eyes, a twisted leg, a scar on a maligned cheek like an apple cut by a thumbnail. There is a balance to be kept. I make the unwhole whole, but . . .

The dolls are my way of being different. A delicate rebellion. They are my way of handling energies that I don't understand, electric energies which course like wine and neon through me, wailing like trains in my arms and chest.

"There are hotels," she said, and laughed, a stuttering sound like a bird trapped in a box. "Maybe if we walk down to . . ." she named a street unfamiliar to me. She wore a man's blue and red checkered work shirt with the cuffs open, jeans and unisex loafers worn down at the sides.

We walked for a couple of blocks. She scuffed one of her feet, a sound that magnified and made the late evening silence almost ominous. We both, I'm certain, felt ridiculous in the company of the other. I was wearing brown slacks, freshly cleaned and creased, a pastel shirt and a brown corduroy jacket. Nondescript, straight, I have always felt that pastels provided me with anonymity, a privacy that I craved as much as Janis feasted on spotlights and crowds. We fought about my image. Slowly I have let go. I have let my hair grow; had it styled. I wear faded jeans and a Pierre Cardin shirt, and hand-tooled boots and belt of leather soft and warm as sundrenched moss.

"Do you think we're getting closer to downtown or farther away?" I asked.

"I don't know." There was an ice-cream store across the street, closed of course, a pink neon cone blinked in the window.

"I have a room."

"Where?"

I named the hotel.

"I don't know it." I fished the key out of my jacket pocket. We checked the address on the oxblood tag, our heads together under a streetlight. Neither of us knew where it was. It was there that we exchanged names. Close to her, I discovered about her the odor of peaches ripe in the sun. I remembered visiting my grandmother in summer, walking in a peach orchard near Wenatchee in the Willamette Valley in Washington where the peaches lay like copper coins on the grass, where the distant-engine drone of wasps filled the air as they sucked away the flesh from the fallen fruit. As they did, the peach scent thickened making the air soft and sweet as a first kiss. Walking in San Francisco that night was like stepping among peach petals.

"Perhaps if I get a taxi," I said, looking around. The street was dark in all directions.

"I've never done this before," Janis said, and leaned against me, taking my hand, hers rough and dry as cardboard.

"I believe you," I said. We both laughed then. Hers less nervous now, coarse and throaty, full of barrooms and stale beer.

"I mean, I've propositioned guys before, but no one ever took me up on it. They practically walked right through me like I was fucking invisible."

"Everyone has to start someplace," I said inanely.

"When we get to the top of the hill we'll be able to tell by the lights where downtown is," Janis said.

"Or we could look for moss on the north side of utility poles?"

"You're weird," she said, and I could see, as the golden tines of streetlight touched her face, that she had thousands of freckles. "Gimme a cigarette."

"I don't have any . . . I don't smoke."

"I don't suppose you'd have a drink on you either?"

"No."

"You're sure you want a girl?" and her mouth widened into a beautiful grin as she held my hand tighter and we both laughed. "Where you from?"

"Iowa."

"They grow corn there don't they? A state full of corn farmers. Are you a corn farmer?"

"No. I repair dolls." I looked quizzically at her to see how she'd react.

"No shit? That's weird, man. You're funny. I don't mean queer funny. Well, maybe I do. No, I think funny, funny. You are, aren't you?"

"And you," I said, "where do you come from?"

"About fifteen miles from Louisiana," she said, and it was her turn to look at me with lifted eyebrows.

"I don't understand," I said.

"You don't need to. It's a private joke," and she paused. "I sing a little." We had reached the top of the hill. "Hey, we are going in the right direction. When we get down to the lights we can ask somebody how to get to that hotel of yours."

But before we went to the hotel she wanted to go to a bar. "There's this joint I know. It's downstairs and there isn't a window in the place. I love it. It's always the same time there . . . no night or day . . . it's like being closed up in a bottle of water . . . time just stands still . . ."

I looked at her, scruffy as a tomcat, but radiating the same kind of pride.

It was a forlorn bar, a dozen stools and a few wooden tables. A place that looked as if it had endured a century of continuous Monday nights. There was a red exit sign above a bandstand where a lonely guitar leaned against a yellowed set of drums.

Old men dozed at the tables, a woman with straight gray hair, dressed in a man's tweed topcoat, glared angrily into a beer. A black man, looking like a failed basketball player, drunk or drugged, lolled crazily on a bar stool. A sampling of Janis's favorite people.

"I understand them," she says.

She has infinite patience with drunks. She'll listen to their stupid convoluted ramblings as they whine about how badly the world has treated them.

"I've been there. I'd be there now if I hadn't met you."

Janis, when she was drunk, had her own sad story. "The Famous Story of the Saturday Night Swindle," she called it, and depending upon her mood the story could take up to an hour to tell. Condensed, it was simply that all our lives we are conditioned to expect a good time Saturday night, we look forward to it and plan for it. And almost always we are disappointed. Yet we keep on trying for there will always be another Saturday night.

In the winter, her freckles become pale, seem to sink just below the surface of her skin like trout in a shallow stream. In summer they multiply: dandelions on a spring lawn. "Fuck, look at me; I look like I've been dipped in Rice Krispies."

"I love your freckles," I say. "Each and every one of them. I am turned on by freckles," and I hold her, kissing slowly across her cheeks and nose.

I love to watch the light in the eyes of little girls as they retrieve their dolls from me. In my workroom I have a row of shoe-box hospital beds. I have painted brown bed-ends on the apple green wall above each box. On the front of each box is a make-believe medical chart. The wall glows with flowered decals and sunny happy-faces. Sometimes, if I have to order parts all the way from Baltimore, I let the children visit their dolls for a while on Saturday afternoons.

My own children are like dolls, girls, all angel eyes and soft little kisses. Cory, my wife, makes their clothes. We walk to church each Sunday down the heavily treed streets of white houses. Our home is surrounded and overpowered by lilacs. There is a groaning porch swing where we sit in the liquid summer dusk. Even in the humid summers Cory always wears a sweater, usually a pale pink or blue, pulled tight across her shoulders as if it were a shield that might protect her.

"What'll it be?" the bartender asked as we settled on the stools.

"Kentucky Red," said Janis.

"The same," I shrugged. I had no idea what I was ordering. The bartender had a flat face with a permanent case of razor burn, and short hair that he might have cut himself with a bowl and a mirror.

"I'm afraid I'm gonna turn out like that," Janis said, inching closer to me by shifting her weight on the bar stool. She nodded toward the shaggy old woman sitting alone and hostile, a cigarette burning toward her fingers. "I'm afraid I'm gonna be one of them loud old women who wear heavy stockings all year and slop from bar to bar getting drunker and more cantankerous by the minute. I don't want to, but the writing's on the fucking wall," she said, hefting her glass.

I moved myself closer to her. I have an abiding fear of old men who sit in bars and hotel lobbies, brittle and dry as insects mounted under glass. I thought of my hotel, decaying on a sidehill, an ancient facade decorated like a fancy wedding cake, a brown linoleum floor in a lobby full of old men and dying ferns.

Janis tossed back her second drink. I pushed mine toward her, barely touched.

"You ain't a juicer?" she said and grinned.

"Should we go look for the hotel?" I said. I was feeling edgy. Perhaps she only wanted a mark to buy her drinks and cigarettes.

"You mean you still want to?" she said, surprised. She eyed me warily, like a dog that had been kicked too many times. "I mean, man, you seen me in some light, and you've been with me long enough to make up your mind . . ."

"I still want to."

Deep in the night I turned over, away from Janis, but with no intention of leaving the bed. She grasped at my arm, much the same as she had grasped at my sleeve earlier in the evening.

"Don't fucking leave me, man." I moved back closer to her. "You any idea what it's like to wake up in the middle of the night alone and know that there ain't a person in the whole fucking world who cares if you live or die? You feel so useless . . ." And she held me fiercely, crying, kissing, trying to pull me close enough to heal her wounds—fuse me to her—store my presence for the lonely nights she anticipated.

Years later, Janis at Woodstock, blue her favorite color, blue her chosen mood—anxiety nibbling at her like rats before she went onstage. But the magical change in her as she did: like throwing an electric switch in her back; she pranced onstage stoned in mind and body by whatever evil she could stab into

131

her veins or gulp into her stomach. Footwork like a boxer, waving the microphone phallically in front of her mouth— blue shades, blue jacket, blue toreador pants, sweating booze, blind, barefoot, she spun like an airplane. She made history onstage. She collapsed into my arms as she came off.

"Sweet Jesus, but I was awful."

"You were a wonder."

"I'll never be able to appear in public again." She holds me like the end of the world. She is wet with sweat and pants into my shoulder while I tell her again and again how great she was. Finally she relaxes. I have done my job.

"Yeah? You really want to? How about that," and she smiled like a kid. "Harry?" she said to the bartender, "is it okay?" and she nodded toward the tiny, dark stage.

"Sure, Janis," he replied. "You know you're welcome any time."

Her music: like a woman making a declaration of love with a fishbone caught in her throat. All the eerie beauty and lone- liness of the Northern Lights. Like getting laid, lovingly and well. That is what the critics said about her.

How to explain her success? Voyeurism? Vicarious living? The world likes to watch people bleed, suffer and die. Janis stands up onstage and metaphorically slits her wrists while the audience says, "Yeah! Man, that's the way I feel. That's what I want to do, but don't have the nerve."

She opens her chest and exposes her heartbeat like a bloody strobe light, and they watch and they scream and they stomp and have wet dreams and climax as they stand on their chairs and say, "Man, that was wonderful. But I'm glad it's her and not me."

"Why on earth do you want to go to San Francisco?" my mother said to me when I told her of my decision to holiday on the west coast. "Why go way out there? California is full of strange people." She was wearing a gray-hen-colored housedress, a kerchief on her hair, her gold-rimmed glasses sparking in the bright kitchen light.

"I'd like to see some strange people."

"Well, your daddy and I went to St. Louis on our honeymoon. Saw the site of the World's Fair and your daddy went to see the St. Louis Browns play baseball, though I'll never understand why. Goodness knows that team never won a game to my recollection."

In the bar again the next evening, Janis a little drunk. "Jesus, don't keep looking at me like that."

"I'm sorry."

"You're a gawker. They're the worst kind. You must spend your life looking over fences and through windows. What's the matter with me? You look like the creeps I went to school with. What the fuck are you doing with a sleazy chick like me?"

"I like you," I said lamely.

"Cheap thrills . . . you can go back to . . . wherever, and tell your fucking dolls about the weird chick you balled in San Francisco. Everybody who looks weird gets fucked over . . . did you know that? I been fucked over so many times. Mostly by guys I don't want. But by the ones I want to. Shit, I been turned down more times than the bedspread in a short-time room."

And on and on, and I listen and shrug it off, for I understand her, and I sense that when she goes after me with words sharp as a gutting knife, that she is really slashing at herself. If she can make me hate her, then I'll leave her and she'll be alone, the way she feels she deserves to be.

She is so unlike Cory. Janis protects herself with loud words, loud music, loud colors, clouds of feathers and jangling bracelets, but they could be twins; each of their bodies is riddled with fear.

Cory: tiny and gentle. Afraid of the world. Cory loves me. I love her as carefully as if she were flower petals or fine china.

Our loving is silent, unlike with Janis who screams and moans and thrashes and tries to absorb my very body into hers. Cory is a broken doll, an abused child, battered, raped, bartered, reviled. She clings to me in her silence. Her climax is barely a shiver. That first night in the hotel Janis shrieked as if she were onstage, a note, clear and sharp as a tuning fork, hung in the air of that sad hotel as her body fairly exploded beneath me.

The only place Janis is not afraid is on the stage. Bracelets splashing lights like diamonds, she high-steps to the microphone and begins her cooing, growling, guttural delivery. She is the spirit of Bessie Smith, Billie Holiday, and every gritty, gutsy blues singer who ever wailed. There is a sensuality, a sexuality, in the primeval sounds she emits. There is terror, love, sex, passion, pain, but mainly sex.

"I sound like I'm in heat," she said to an interviewer once, "and baby, I am. Sometimes I go right from the stage and I pick up my honey here," she said, referring to me, "and we go right to the hotel and ball, and ball, and ball."

"I sing right from my pussy," she said another time, then pulled her blue sunglasses down on her nose so she could peek over them to get the full shocked reaction.

"Why did you choose to sing?" an interviewer once asked her.

"It was a way out," she replied. "Where I come from a girl works at catching a man—then has a lot of kids and keeps her mouth shut. I'm hyper . . . I've always been like a pan of boiling water."

"Do you know what the difference is?" I asked Janis as she clung to me after a concert, sobbing, repeating over and over how awful she had been . . . *awful*, after fifteen thousand people had danced in the aisles and screamed out their love for her. "The difference between what you do and what I used to do is that mine, and almost everyone else's work, is tangible. I'd build a house or a garage or even repair a doll and when I was finished I could say, 'There is the house I built or the doll

I've repainted.' You have to wait to be evaluated. You sing a song or record an album but it means nothing until the fans buy or the critics say, 'Yes, this is good.' "

It takes very special people to bare their souls for mere humans to evaluate. Not many can stand up to it. I have always tried to remember that when I find Janis drunk or stoned— when she rages and accuses and smashes, and vomits, and lies in a fitful sleep, sweat on her upper lip and forehead, her mouth agape.

My assignment, as I sometimes look upon it, has been to protect Janis from herself and from people: those who would tap her veins and draw the life from her like so many vampires with straws. I am known as the most protective manager in the business. We hardly ever tour anymore. There are the albums and Janis plays Vegas for twelve weeks a year.

Has it been worth it? Has what I've gone through been worth it to prolong a career for a few more years? In just a month or two it's going to happen. I will go home to Iowa, alone, "for a holiday," I'll say. But I'll know differently. Janis will be left alone in the house near Las Vegas: that desert house, arid and dry as Janis's hands the night we met. A twenty-thousand-dollar boat stands like the mythical, mystical ark, on a trailer in the back driveway. The nearest lake is sixty miles away and artificially created. Janis bought the boat like anyone else would buy a Tonka Toy as a gift for a child. We have never used it. I stare at it and shudder.

While I am away, the mouse will play, and play, and play. And she will finish doing what I interrupted in San Francisco, what she has been trying to do all her life, not maliciously, or viciously, or violently, but with that lack of care, of restraint, that has always characterized her.

Fog is heavy in my life, dimensions of time telescope—I have been called. I have given nearly twenty years of my life for ten of hers. But no one knows. Really knows. There are other dimensions where Janis no longer exists, where I never left Iowa, where I sit tonight on a white front porch in the humid dusk and string my dolls.

"Nobody ever stays with me," Janis said in the gray morning light of my creaking hotel room.

"I'll stay as long as I can," I said.

"How long is that?" And I couldn't bring myself to answer. My flight home was booked for the next afternoon.

"You know, just the sound of your voice, even if you're talking about dolls, is more to me than solid food. I just get so fucking lonely."

"Nobody likes to be alone."

"Was I crying last night?"

"A little."

"More than that wasn't it? I do that when I get drunk. I cried on your shoulder, right?"

"You weren't any trouble."

"Thanks for staying with me. I mean, really."

We walked the warm morning streets for a while, small clouds were low enough to touch, still as the foggy gulls perched on posts along the piers. We breakfasted at a squalid café. Again we sat on stools at the counter. An oriental, wrapped tight as a mummy in a filthy white apron, was cook and waiter. I ordered bacon and eggs. Good, solid, nutritious North American food. Janis had pecan pie, ice cream and a Coke. Junkie food I was to learn later as my education progressed. She grinned at me through the widening haze of her Marlboro.

"I'm sorry you're not staying."

"So am I."

"Well, I'll move on," she said, sliding off the stool. "Maybe I'll see you around . . ."

"You're not going to leave," I said. "I don't have to go until tomorrow."

"You mean you *want* to stay with me? I'm grateful you stayed last night . . . you don't have to put yourself out."

"I want to stay with you."

"But you have to go back to . . . Iowa."

"I have a job to get back to . . . and my dolls."

"F'chrissakes."

"I have to . . . I'm sorry."

"Still, it's weird though, a big man like you messing with dolls."

An eight-inch steel implement that looks like a large crochet hook is the main tool of my trade; accessories consist of a supply of sturdy elastics, glue, a teakettle, a set of pastel paints. Exposure to a steaming teakettle allows me to soften joints and remove arms, legs and heads. Like Dr. Christiaan Barnard I perform transplants. Like the good Dr. Frankenstein, I have a box of leftover parts from which I often extract a leg or an eye to make a broken doll good as new.

When we reached the room, we were both perilously shy, Janis even slightly reluctant. The exchange of money was forgotten. "Are you sure?" Janis asked several times, still expecting to be rejected.

"I am," I reassured, though I wondered why. She was so opposite to the girls I knew at home. I couldn't explain my excitement, my desire for this plain, shoddily dressed, rather vulgar girl. Perhaps even then I felt the charisma. I never confused her with her singing. I wanted her before she ever sang to me. But there was that power about her. She has the ability to stand onstage and hold the audience as if she were whispering in the ear of a lover, or lead them to dance in the aisles, or stand on the tables and stomp out her rhythms like a biker putting boots to a cop.

"You know what they did to me? At the university I was voted 'Ugliest Man On Campus.' You any idea what that did to me? Those straight chicks in angora sweaters and skirts, lipstick, and about a ton of hairspray, and the guys in cords and sweaters, or even shirts and ties . . . and just because I was different . . ."

I had asked about her former life. Sometimes I try to learn the why of her, but gently, like unwinding gauze from a wound. Years have passed and she trusts me now, as much as she ever trusts anyone. I never made my flight back to Iowa. Have never left her. I paid for my parents to visit us once. Only once.

"Your workshop's just as you left it," my mother said. "I just closed up the door. Had to take the sign down eventually . . . Little girls kept coming to the house."

"Oh, they thought they were so fucking righteous. But I'll show them. I can buy and sell them all now. I showed them once. I'm gonna show them for the rest of my life. They all married each other and live in the city and have split-level plastic houses, and plastic kids, and cars, and cocks, and cunts . . ." and she broke off amid a mixture of laughter and tears. "I suppose I should be happy just not to be part of them anymore . . . be happy being different . . . shit, it was only fifteen miles to Louisiana, and that was where the real people were, and real music. That was where I did my first gigs, and learned how to drink, and yeah, that too. God, did I ever tell you about high school? What they did to me? You don't want to hear, Sugar. It was too awful to even talk about."

"Are you sorry?" Janis once asked me, in a strange soft voice, as if she had suddenly had a glimpse through the veil at what could have been: at what life would have been like if we hadn't met.

"I miss handling nails in the sunshine—the raw strength in my arms. My hands would blister now if I really worked."

"And your dolls."

"I miss them too."

"You know, I've never seen you fix a doll. I bet you were good. I've told you you could . . ."

"It wouldn't be the same."

"Maybe when we're old?"

"Maybe."

The third morning. The same café. Our going there a fragile attempt at ritual.

"Do you need anything?" I was reaching for my wallet.

"Hell, no. I'll get by. I always do. I'm just as tough as I look. Tougher." We walked out of the café hand in hand.

She turned to me then to be kissed. A shy, hurried brushing of lips, our bodies barely touching. About us, the beautiful scent of peaches.

"Be cool. Maybe I'll see you around," and she gave me the peace sign, something I'd never seen before, and shambled away among the moving crowd.

Here, on the lazy verandah in the Iowa dusk, as my children sleep, as my dolls sleep, as my wife waits with her delicate love, I dream. Am haunted by the spirit of a dead girl. A dead singer who died a broken doll, pitched face-first onto a blondwood night table in a Los Angeles motel. Nose broken, spewing blood, she wedged between the table and the bed, her life ebbing while the needle grinned silver in the darkness. I remember her in my arms in that sad hotel in San Francisco, wild, enveloping, raucous as her songs, her tongue like a wet, sweet butterfly in my mouth. I am haunted by her death and by what might have been. And what I might have done to prevent her rendezvous with the needle: surrogate cock. Evil little silver dildo. A sexual partner she didn't have to fear. The needle never left her alone in the middle of the night. I sometimes look at my hands, marveling that there are no wounds, so many times have I pushed the needle away.

"If you can't get love one way—in the physical way—then you get it in another," she said to me during those fine days we spent together before it all began. During the few gigs she'd done she had discovered that the applause, screams, cheers, wails, were enough for then. "I'm only somebody when I sing, but God, the gigs are so few and far between." Of course, that was to change, and soon.

Friends were visiting Cory and me the night that Janis's death was announced. It was an afterthought item at the end of the news, between weed killer and fertilizer commercials.

"Oh," was all Cory said.

"Who?" said my parents.

"Who?" said our friends, noting my consternation. *She* watches the soap operas in the afternoons. *He* collects records of marching bands.

After our first breakfast we walked all day, looked at the ocean, the terraced houses frosty white as splashes of tropic sun. The day was full of spring—all San Francisco tasted and smelled of peaches.

The magic of her—whirling onto the stage—a white girl singing black music—the trills, the shrieks, the croaks, the moans, as she made love through her music. "The only love I know is with the audience—that's my whole life," she told an interviewer once, as I shrank into the shadows. But the gods of music would have been pleased with her, "a whirling dervish with blue nail polish, a wall of hair closing over her face like drapes," is how *Rolling Stone* described her recently. "The biggest, wildest, roughest, most flawed diamond in show business." We have sold more records than anyone but Elvis.

The picture-taking session over, Janis, exhausted, rests her head on my shoulder. "Sweet Jesus, but I need a drink."

"Just one," I say, and she makes a face at me, shaking her head.

"Aw, Sugar, after a session like that Mama needs to cut loose."

"We'll see," I say as we walk off the set.

I think of all the people that her life touched in the sixties and until her death: all those people whose lives are different in countless tiny and not so tiny ways because I appeared to Janis on a dark San Francisco street on a spring night.

I can't help but wonder how much of history I have personally changed. I know what is going to happen soon but am powerless to stop it, not even sure that I would if I could. In my workshop a few swatches of blue satin, a dozen lion-colored hairs, a few feathers and rhinestones . . .

About
the
Author

W. P. KINSELLA is best known for his award-winning novel *Shoeless Joe*, which became the film *Field of Dreams* in 1989. His other books include *The Iowa Baseball Confederacy*, *The Fencepost Chronicles*, *The Miss Hobbema Pageant*, and his most recent book, *Box Socials*. A native Canadian, Kinsella earned a B.A. at the University of Victoria and an M.F.A. at the University of Iowa. He and his wife, Ann Knight, live in White Rock, British Columbia.